a love story

RELAPSE

a love story

ROBERT HUNTER

— Beaver's Pond Press —

Minneapolis, MN

Edited by Margaret Wright

Proofread by Leonard Pierce of Kevin Anderson & Associates

Managing Editor: Hanna Kjeldbjerg

ISBN: 978-1-59298-704-7

Library of Congress Catalog Number: 2018900262

Printed in the United States of America

First Printing: 2018

22 21 20 19 18   5 4 3 2 1

Book design by Athena Currier

Beaver's Pond Press, Inc.
7108 Ohms Lane
Edina, MN 55439–2129

(952) 829-8818

www.BeaversPondPress.com

To order, visit www.ItascaBooks.com or call 1-800-901-3480 ext. 118.
Reseller discounts available.

To Becky,
Maybe reality was never meant for the likes of us in the first place.
I've moved on to fiction.
Love, Rob

Chapter 1

I WAS SITTING IN A COUNSELOR'S OFFICE when the heart palpitations returned. They were no minor contractions. I gasped for breath. But before the counselor could call 911, I settled myself to avoid any uniformed interference, and for the sake of therapeutic insight.

It was late October, and cold enough in central Pennsylvania to freeze truck tires solid in inch-thick mud. Everything was petrified except the crushing whitewater in the Lehigh River Gorge. It had been a most insufferable season for reasons I could explain, having seen the consequences of my wandering from one tumultuous relationship to another. And then, just when it seemed I finally had a solid sense of direction, there came another twist. It sent me temporarily sideways like a love-lost paddler caught in a backwash. I was searching for a safe outlet.

The counselor's name was Marie. I began telling her about what was weighing on my mind as it pertained to the crisis at hand, except she was too young and blonde and fragile for the unmitigated truth. I'm a good judge of character, which is a part of my natural instinct as a writer.

I told her about the story I'd been working on—and about Annie Cotner, the woman I married who lured me to Maine under false pretenses, subjecting me to torment and great peril. It was imperative for Marie to understand that I had seen this coming to some degree. It would explain why I'd read Annie's journal: not solely out of curiosity, but to protect myself from the forces I sensed were closing in.

Marie was taking notes.

"Raft guides, for one thing, can never be trusted," I said.

In my defense, I am not suspicious or hateful by nature. I'd been put through an emotional wringer against my will, and my weaknesses for wild women and alcohol made me an easy target. The whole experience would've flattened a lesser, more sober man. So affliction itself was a form of unnatural catharsis—not that I was to blame. But not once in my previous marriage had I been forced to resort to that degree of subterfuge.

Annie was a closed book. She had a history I could sense—when not fully preoccupied with my own suffering and with securing further mateship in the shortest possible amount of time. Admittedly, six months isn't long enough for proper vetting, however honed one's instinct; which was why I had to investigate, in an effort to expedite the process and for the benefit of all parties involved.

"Then I knew *too* much," I told Marie, and furthermore, it clouded my judgment and impacted the quality of my writing, which made life intolerable.

By the time I'd resorted to pathetic white-coat therapy, I'd already exhausted all other forms, including prescription medications in experimental doses, which were not quite as remedial as you'd imagine. Reading Annie's journal under the influence one night may have, in fact, been the tipping point that not only inspired my subsequent investigations, but also the wayward trip to Maine and everything after, which had finally rendered me fully frozen and otherwise useless.

Suicide had been a last resort.

In the meantime, I counted on alcohol to get me through and to spur the creative process. It never made me angry or led me toward any dubious intent that I knew of. It helped me write.

I learned to drink as a matter of ritual, formerly in my old studio while Kelsey, my ex, sang and played piano horribly. Kelsey was a beautiful creature not born of this world, a mystic witch with uncommon powers of percipience and persuasion. She was an alcoholic love song, and so she mostly didn't mind my drinking. Moreover, and more often, she supplied the sauce; and for that I'd loved her, in spite of herself.

She was the one who convinced me to take the job in sales at Stager Auto World and impelled me to keep hold of it for her own selfish reasons even after it'd begun to stifle my cleverness. I bought her the upright with my first commission check, which was a mistake. The music eventually drove me to madness. I began drawing characters in stories just to spite her, and she ended up hating me because it was brilliant, and too true to be fiction. She would say, "You're writing about me again, you miserable bastard! Your writing is terrible. *You're* terrible!" And I would emphatically deny this, once pointing to the unfamiliar names of characters on the pages she'd crumpled up as evidence of my virtue. "You've only rearranged the letters!" she exclaimed.

And so, having underestimated her intellect as well as her commitment to playing the piano, I drank in greater quantity, citing writer's block. The waking hours got shorter, and eventually, in a fit of anxious rage, I pulled a pistol from the closet, loaded the barrel, and fired six shots through the side of that cheap Falcone while she was away. This was last August. After that, everything got much worse before there was any sign that life would get better.

Marie could only assure me that everything would work out for the best.

There is only so much they can teach you about insight for free at a junior college, which was how I ended up in sales to keep the bills paid. And dear Marie ended up here on a Saturday morning with her clipboard and JCPenney blouse, trying to grow therapeutic roots in the face of all aridity. I'd noticed her Lackawanna County Community College certificate, *L tre C* as locals called it, hung proudly on her wall. I sympathized, knowing there was no hope to be found as far as any therapeutic reconciliation was concerned, because we were prodigal underachievers, and I told her the universe had conspired against us.

"Life is continual suffering," I said. "And no matter what we think, say, or try to conjure up, it makes no difference at all."

Perhaps there is no such thing as providence in a world so utterly hapless.

Marie raised an eyebrow and smiled sympathetically. This was all the poor girl's limited experience would allow. I hated to break it to her. She had obviously never been to Maine, and she didn't know Annie. This was uncharted territory, but I knew if I was going to find any clarity on the matter whatsoever, I'd better tread lightly so as not to get locked up as a knee-jerk reaction to what I had to say.

"Should I continue on?" I asked.

"Oh yes, please do," Marie replied.

She seemed intrigued and wanted to help me weigh all the options. To that extent, in my mind, few remained.

♦ ♦ ♦

Annie and I were living in an old house, owned by her father, at their farm in Hazard, Pennsylvania. Last fall, Lee Donegan, a river guide and old friend of Annie's, was our houseguest. The place was a bastion for mongrels, planted amidst eighty acres of plowable earth that no one bothered to sow. No one besides Annie and her father, Dirk, knew the reason why nothing spotless flourished there. I didn't care, so long as the strawberry wine held out and I could occasionally write unfettered in blissful, meditative silence.

But I'd forgotten what vile and horrible creatures some men have the propensity to be, as wily as the filthy strays that screeched and screwed at night in the shrubs outside our bedroom window. Annie never realized it. She seemed to prefer the scruffy ones, and could tell just by the sound one would make when it found what it was looking for, tucked up and hissing beneath the arborvitae.

"Don't you just want to bring them inside?" she asked one night, battling with her apparently inborn compulsion to take in anything with mange.

She began to say that life was becoming especially mundane on the farm and first mentioned taking the trip to Maine when I fell over onto the bed from drunkenness and heard the cat she called Sunny begin to whine.

I said, "That thing is a damn deviant!"

Annie looked at me, offended. I told her I was just delirious and always prone to excessive personification whenever her father brought out the wine.

Earlier that night I'd helped him drink it, as was often the case, in an effort to fight the cold and despair. Dirk was a beastly, large man with wild philosophies to match the tanglements in his long gray hair and beard. To him it was all very serious, those mad drunk theories combining aliens and religion.

"Didn't you see that documentary?" he asked me.

I told Dirk I hadn't. He scoffed and pulled the cork on another homemade bottle.

"This is sweet red," he told me, which is pure alcohol by any other account or in any other vintage but his. We drank as Dirk rambled on.

"You believe in God, don't you?" he asked.

I told him I did.

"Well, God is just a metaphor for all the knowledge we've gained as a people, a civilization," he said. "And God came from the sky, right? Every culture has catalogued that in one way or another: cave drawings, Indian folklore, the Scriptures . . . ,"

"Yes . . . yes," I said.

I was too fascinated and afraid to argue, or interject, or say anything, even if I had any reason to disagree.

"You know, in God we've discovered the truth," he said, continuing on, "that there is another side."

"Yes, of course," I replied. This was not a revelation, but more an attempt, in a rare moment of unified understanding, to fit the construct of what I learned to believe in Sunday school into his mad, conspiratorial dogma.

I knew Leona, Annie's mother, had died suddenly years ago from complications during labor. A bout with cancer and the supposed cure, chemotherapy, had weakened her heart substantially, and Aiden was never born. I assumed this was the reason for Dirk trying to rationalize the other, more eminent God of the Bible. He emphatically denied His existence because of harbored resentment, visions he had, and other circumstantial evidence he considered proof that alien life-forms were in charge.

"You know, Leona is still here," he explained. He said she'd taken on many forms now, and I believed him. The crickets nearby, who'd chirped all along in protest of our late night elucidations, suddenly fell silent.

Lee Donegan, our raft guide boarder—unwelcomed and uninvited where I was concerned—was over at our house with Annie, watching my television, so I stayed even longer than normal, listened and laughed along with Dirk, and drank his wine until we both forgot what the problem was, and it all made sense.

Then came a sad, silent realization. All the wine was gone, so I knew it was time for us to retire and save the rest of the conversation for later.

I texted Annie, who was soon there to help me stumble home, as she often did. We made our way over ruts carved in a steep dirt path, through the weeds and thicket. Dirk claimed to have built the house with his own two hands, and it'd cost him a fortune, which was supposed to explain why the rent I paid him for such a tiny ranch house seemed so high.

"I don't know about your father," I kidded Annie, who by then was practically forced to carry me over her shoulders.

She said Dirk was never the same after her mother passed, and the farm died along with her. Annie called it *blight*. I knew nothing about farming, but the term matched exactly the one I'd have used, so I squeezed her broad hay-hauling shoulders tightly to let her know I understood. When we got inside, Lee was sitting in the living room, petting a gray stray on his lap. Two others sat defiantly atop the mute upright piano, which I'd been awarded in the divorce along with the flat screen exclusively. Annie pulled out a few bowls and began filling them with cat food. My desk was now an old kitchen table, piled high with Lee's ever-growing stack of things, including a musty, stinking life preserver that I promptly flung to the floor. I clumsily tried to clear a corner for writing as Annie went for a quick shower and got ready for bed.

Lee confided in me at that point that his plans to move back to West Virginia had fallen through. He had no other place to go.

"The Gauley River situation is a fucking mess," he said. Some tourist googans went under and their families blamed the guide service for negligence, so he said he might have to stay "for the duration." Or at least until they found the bodies.

"Did you talk to Annie about this?" I asked.

Lee said his staying there was her idea.

Then it was clear, even having not yet read the journal but under significant pressure from encroachment, that I must ramp up the pace of my courtship. I'd make an all-out effort to win Annie over with exclusivity, if for no other reason than to secure a form of sanctity for writing fiction in my otherwise bankrupt existence.

By then it was after midnight. Annie was upstairs, so I joined her with full intent to solidify and consummate our tenuous affair by whatever means necessary. Moments later we were back to arguing about the cats, which led to my implicating Lee and possibly others for not having our best interests at heart, amongst other things. In those days this was all conjecture, of course, and she categorically refuted my more outrageous claims. I agreed to drop it.

"But I'm calling an exterminator for the fleas!" I exclaimed. Annie recoiled.

"And what about you?" she roared back, now on the offensive.

"What about me?"

"You must think I'm blind!"

She then dreamed up some sinister scenario where I maintained a cordial relationship with my ex as a backup plan. I acknowledged nothing as she laid out her case, except that I had spoken to Kelsey infrequently and only when necessary in the settlement of official state-sponsored decrees.

In my current state of knacker, I saw no clear path to forbearance. I had no sins to parlay so far as Kelsey was concerned, and I furthermore understood that she had already shacked up with a new boyfriend in Allentown, with monies derived from my continued employment at the car dealership.

"The whole matter is settled," I assured Annie. And anyway, I'd further caught wind of Kelsey having purchased a brand new keyboard. At least Annie didn't sing, and there was the novel to take into consideration.

"I think you have a lot to learn about women," Annie said.

My buzz began to fade.

I knew this was all simply a ploy to disrupt my efforts to undermine Lee and those of his persuasion. Whose side was she on?

After some time, Annie forgave my aberrance because she believed it was destiny that we should be together. I forgave her also, because it was late and I had no better plan in mind. I had to work in six hours to keep a roof over everyone's head, including Lee's, the treacherous raft guide who, I had yet to discover by reading Annie's memoirs, had been much more than a friend, as she'd always maintained.

Annie joined me on the bed and sprawled herself out half-naked to confess her love for me. Her divine expression was thoroughly beguiling. And so, suddenly unaware of all other considerations, I said I loved her too.

I was also still determined to prove it.

When she again mentioned the Maine excursion, I instantly agreed to go.

I knew Lee must have heard her joyful shrieks from downstairs. It's the mark of a great writer to be able to perform in any condition. Then Annie asked what I was thinking, but I had nothing clever to say. In light of everything, I was ill-prepared to proffer up a prospectus, or any other alternative besides bondship, that could lead toward the future I envisioned—one without life preservers cluttering up my desk. So I asked her to marry me, imagining I could finally quit my day job at Stager Auto World, work odd jobs on the farm, and finally compose the great novel I'd been telling people about for years.

Annie gasped and said yes without as much convincing as it took to sanctify Kelsey—and without the prerequisite stipulation that I maintain gainful employment in spite of other wanton literary ambitions. None of those aspirations, of course, had anything to do with either one of them in my mind, except that I found it imperative as a writer, and as a basic human necessity, to share new experiences with others and occasionally sleep with them.

With that outlook in view, I saw no reason for delay. Seven days later, we were sworn in by Carl, the Carbon County justice, in his office, in a most unromantic ceremony surrounded by faux wood paneling and pro-right-wing militaria.

"The wildflowers were a nice touch," Annie said.

She looked so beautiful standing beside the American flag. As we recited our vows, the irises she held perfectly matched the depth I saw in her bright blue eyes. She set the flowers down to place her right hand over her heart, and I followed suit in an impromptu Pledge of Allegiance at the bequest of our officiate. I wasn't sure whether it was appropriate to kiss the bride or salute Carl at the conclusion of the ceremony, so to err on the side of caution I did both.

"God bless America!" said Carl.

I thanked him for his service as we walked out the door.

Lee had already moved on by the time we got back to the farm. Dirk said it had everything to do with the nuptials. Before he left, Lee had stopped at Dirk's house asking for a supply of alcohol and calling me a no-good snake.

"How impudent!" I exclaimed.

"Love is a powerful drug," Dirk replied.

"You didn't give him any of the wine, did you?"

Dirk assured me that he hadn't, and he promised to "relocate" all the other strays at my bequest, except Sunny, who Annie insisted we keep.

After that, many things seemed possible, though I was at all times conflicted and trying to solve mysteries or write them without many clues about what the universe had in store when it led me to Stager Auto World and then back to Hazard at the end of each long day. But there was at least possibility, and stronger libation, if little besides the setting had actually changed since my breakup with Kelsey. I tried not to overthink it.

I'd sworn that conflict was my disease, and that it wasn't purely driven by spite, but a consequence of tense negotiations on the car lot. I blamed those miserable fucks for everything. They deserved it. But my penchant for unabashed aberration and perpetual broken-heartedness ran much deeper, I knew. As far back as childhood, I can recall having a desire to express myself and set the record straight. I found this very often skewed my perception of things, but sometimes made for interesting conversation, especially with Dirk and a bottle of wine. In fact, that was the lure of life on the Cotner farm—a most unapologetic renaissance and renewal—and part of the reason why I'd chosen to stay.

I considered writing to be my only shot at finding redemption and lasting contentment, and the freedom that would come along with knowing that I'd at last searched and suffered long enough to call myself an author. I assumed that's how it would be if I could only begin moving the blue-black Stager ballpoint brilliantly across the blank page—or come up with a proper outline at least. Then I could justify finally leaving the dealership after fifteen years, or burning it down. I measured the option of living in the world as an unemployed derelict, and the prospect of not finding anything good in it, against my former (and in some ways, current) situation—working for minimum commissions and having almost no hope at all.

Annie was much more optimistic.

She had the whole Maine trip mapped out. She'd told me about Dave, who shot a record bull moose, Tabitha's lesbian wedding that was supposed to take place, and the rest of them, whose names were never important to me because raft guides are all the same. I refused to call it a honeymoon. So I made love to her each night when I returned home from work, predicting limited opportunity unless following the scrum.

I had serious reservations, but remained clear-headed enough to commence, once again, with staring at a blank sheet of paper in twilight, hoping for inspiration nightly when my young bride fell asleep. She assured me that the words would come when the time was right. The pursuit of enlightenment, and Annie, consumed me fully thereafter.

Soon she became the subject of both halves of my typically drunk inner narration, lusting after carnal things and curiosities. She embodied them both in a way I had yet to define. It was a wild, blurry ambition, but I had to try.

We set our sights to the North in two sleeps, and stayed up late that night drinking beer, packing, and waiting for it all to begin. Next thing I knew the Jeep was loaded down, and Annie was begging me to leave early. "Screw work," she said. I liked the sound of it, but we had other commitments. Love was in season, I reminded her. My friend Aaron was getting married the next day.

"Oh, shit!" Annie exclaimed.

"My thoughts exactly!" I howled as she rummaged through the hamper filled with dirty clothes for something special to wear.

I decided that if I ever had the balls to do it, I wanted her there for moral support the day I told Paul Stager to fuck off. She was, if nothing else, wild and unafraid of consequence— and beautiful. It was only that, and the prospect of being a writer, which I so desperately wanted, that kept me thoroughly invested, even after reading her journal and knowing the whole truth about her and, by extension, a God whose countenance I never fully trusted either.

Eventually Annie passed out on the couch, exhausted from all her preparations. It was then that I went stumbling down the basement steps in search of more alcohol, already drunk on a combination of Yuengling lager and the anti-anxiety medication I'd been taking. There wasn't much time. I had work in a few hours. So I hurried, found a stock of her father's moonshine right where I'd left it, and sat down to sip amongst the many dusty cardboard boxes piled everywhere. They were all labeled. One said "Journals." I'd bypassed it many times while accessing the stash. I'm not incredulous. I didn't doubt her, necessarily, but there was a lot more at stake now and so many unanswered questions. The eternal bonds of matrimony demand transparency.

The liquor had me feeling Trojan. I honestly couldn't help myself. So I tore in, leafing through pages with packing tape still stuck to my fingers.

What I read I can neither forget, nor forgive myself for reading. It was the unadulterated truth. No wonder Annie kept it from me—though altruism doesn't absolve her of anything. She should have confessed. Maybe then I wouldn't have been so quick to say, "I do."

Then again, Annie should have known that I have a very indulgent nature, especially where questionable judgment is concerned. I can be quite sympathetic given the proper motivation, and might've married her anyways. But I'd have never let Lee Donegan watch my television.

Just then, my morning alarm went off. I silenced the awful sound blaring from my pocket. I was never late for work, no matter my condition. This time I had a momentous reason to be tardy, but Paul Stager wouldn't understand. So I left before the sun came up, as usual, with a holy host of good reasons not to.

I tried talking to my God then, on the long drive in, but He answered only in refrain—perhaps because all of creation had gone totally crazy, and gotten too full and obsessed with disorder and discounts to bother with ministration. I didn't blame Him. If I were in charge, I might watch it burn too.

It's a fucked-up world we live in.

But somehow I knew there'd soon be a sign emanating from the other side, a sign that connected all the blurry, crooked lines. And there'd be impulse and inspiration then too, perhaps—if only I could find a way to phrase it.

Chapter 2

THE CAR BUSINESS IS A SPEED BUMP on the way to hitting rock bottom, which explained what I was still doing at Stager Auto World at dawn with a bad headache. I was recollecting old regrets and new ones with Aaron Turner as he finalized plans for jumping headlong into marriage with a woman named Cynthia Ivey.

"It's not too late," I'd told him as he transferred an assortment of homemade favors from the trunk of a rusty sedan into the cavernous boot at the rear end of a shiny Cadillac plucked straight off the front line.

"It's time we start thinking about the future," he said, but that was all I was thinking of when I suggested we drop everything and drive the black behemoth all the way to Mexico.

"Or possibly Las Vegas on our way to California," I told him. "Just like Captain Wade."

"You told everyone he was crazy," Aaron rebuked.

"Yes, he was. Certifiable. But not for that reason exclusively."

There was nothing sane about working on a car lot in the first place, and no precedent that I knew of for screening any of the throngs of salesmen I'd hired—salesmen who now swarmed the lot in dim dawn light like a coven of gold-chain-wearing vampires. I never checked for signs of pure psychosis before handing over the keys to Paul Stager's bargain kingdom.

Aaron had loved Cynthia in secret up until three months prior. He said she'd saved him from a lifetime of keeping promises that he never should have made. He'd then raised her ringed finger high above our heads on the showroom floor as he simultaneously announced his divorce and engagement to the staff.

"Oh, good God!" exclaimed Paul Stager, who believed in the bonds of matrimony ecclesiastically, even in abominable conditions. I knew he'd later approach me regarding those matters.

He asked that our meeting be kept under the strictest confidence. "Did you know of this?" he questioned after closing his office door and attempting to rub away the stress from his wrinkled brow.

I said, "What a man does in his own time is none of my business."

"Nonsense," said Paul. "This *is* my business." He spilled the coffee he was always carrying down the front of his company polo. "Oh, damn it!" he shouted. "I'm beginning to wonder whose side you're on."

I wasn't sure. Then he asked about last month's numbers.

"They're not bad," I told him, "all things considered." Which was to say, given our lack of management and high-mileage bargain inventory. Worst of all, it was October, the time of year in eastern Pennsylvania when frost covers windshields, helium balloons lose their bounce, and salesmen get desperate.

"Yes, well, we'll have to do worse than that, in this case," he said. "I'm talking about integrity. Morality. Nowadays you can't just fire a man for being a philanderer."

"You must have just cause," I affirmed.

"Of course I know that—and it's just getting worse," he said, insisting there were forces more dubious at play. "What do you know about drugs?"

"Drugs, sir?"

He leaned forward, smoothed his bushy eyebrows, and spoke directly into my face, so close that I could taste the coffee on his breath. "Drugs," he said once again. "That's our best-case scenario, because I wouldn't want to think of the alternative."

Paul liked Aaron, deep down. He needed reliable experience on the floor. His customers demanded it. But he was startled by Aaron's faithless proclamation. It sent him reeling. We discussed rehabilitation. Paul was convinced that one of his own was under the influence of marijuana. What other explanation was there for such an immoral transgression? And I understood "the alternative," the unspeakable beast he often referred to without mentioning his evil name. The specter haunted him like the ghost of some deranged spirit resembling his wife, Peggy. It'd been on his mind ever since Captain Wade Balschi sailed off with one of his weekly specials. But I'd sworn, then and now, that it wasn't madness or possession; that it wasn't just because I'd hired rogue candidates without any merit or discernible skill, simply for my own amusement. So Paul cursed the wacky weed whenever anything went sideways, as it often did—which was fine so long as he wasn't holding me accountable for it, which I very often was.

Nevertheless, Aaron Turner was my friend and the last employee working there who was even close to sane.

I tried reassuring Paul with some of Dirk's wisdom. "Love is a powerful drug," I said. Paul sprang up from his chair and began bold recitations of scripture while Aaron smiled obliviously on the showroom floor.

This was the day of the wedding. By noon, Aaron was frantic, and still trying to load up the Caddy while attempting to explain why there hadn't been a bachelor party as previously discussed. "It's always the same shit with you," he said. He was always missing the point.

"One beer," I insisted.

He said, "You're incapable."

"I'm not," I swore. I called upon him to be the sort of man who keeps promises. "Starting today," I implored as we both climbed aboard the great hulking vessel.

Our khakis slid across slick black leather seats and we were surrounded by wood grain and the smell of stale cigarettes, with our rental tuxes hanging in the backseat. Seconds later, we were roaring through the streets of Hazard, southbound toward Allentown and a blues bar I'd been to before.

"See, it's just down the street," I said.

"Are you sure *this* is the place?" Aaron asked as we pulled up beside the drinkery with a shabby off-white exterior. A group of degenerates stood on the corner getting high in broad daylight. Aaron turned the car off. "One beer," he reiterated. And I could already imagine the look on Paul's face when we both showed up piss-drunk to the unrighteous ceremony, reeking of cigarette smoke and freedom.

One of the men outside wore a faded green jacket with a patch I recognized from the office of the county justice days earlier. He moved toward us, picked up a crushed butt from the sidewalk, and asked Aaron for a light. Aaron recoiled. "Nope," he said indifferently.

"What the fuck is your problem?" I sniped at Aaron. "Can't you see this man is a veteran?"

A man of his prejudice, with lethal training, in the midst of a serious nicotine addiction, as it was, could've snapped our necks in a heartbeat. I held up a match as he straightened out the filter and puffed until smoke poured from the tip and out of his two tremendous, quivering nostrils. Then the man, presumably HENDERSON as the nameplate on his jacket implied, brushed Aaron's bad mojo off his shoulders.

"Hoooo-ra," he said. It felt like I was back in New York the weekend Kelsey kicked Aaron and I both out for debauchery and we'd stopped at every bar in Albany before finding our bearings again in the Adirondack wilds.

We were both still searching as we went inside.

"You know you'd be lost without me, Aaron," I said as we made our way through the loud colorful throngs, like pilgrims in a strange land, straight to the crowded bar. The bartender lady shouted something encouraging over all the noise, and I locked eyes with her. I thought one of hers might have been a glass eye, in fact, and said as much to Aaron as we approached.

"It's his bachelor party," I said and ordered up a double-double.

"Hey, hey," rebuked Aaron in typical dramatic fashion. He threw up his arms, protesting my attempt to celebrate, and inadvertently struck the barmaid silly, jarring the prosthetic orb loose of its moorings.

The eyeball bounced off the filthy, beer-soaked counter and fell to the floor. Aaron lunged instinctively to retrieve it, then lost his nerve and pulled out at the last second without grasping it.

Aaron gagged, then was tossed around by the drunken revelers amidst all the commotion, and I said to the barmaid, "I'm very sorry for my friend."

The barmaid hissed, then laughed insanely, producing an auxiliary prosthetic from a nearby glass to fill the sunken void as the band struck up a baleful chord.

"Good God," Aaron exclaimed, witnessing this.

She handed over the beer and I tipped her heavy for the grief as she began to sway her jet-black hair all around to the music. I figured it was time to sit Aaron down—or sequester him—before he got us into any more trouble.

"All's forgiven," I insisted then, and told him to drink his beer. We found a vacant corner to better accommodate his theatrics, and I tried talking sense into him once again.

"This is exactly what I meant before," he whimpered.

"You can thank me later," I said. "And for God's sake, keep your voice down, or these people are going to think we're a couple of prudes."

"What do you care what these people think?" he asked.

I told him he was totally out of line.

"These people?" I retorted.

"These psychos!" he replied.

I admitted the glass eye scenario was peculiar, but the rest of his complaining, I knew, was a gross overreaction, probably because of stress associated with the wedding. I said getting married again was a bad idea.

"To Annie?" he asked.

I recoiled.

"How dare you say something like that to me," I growled. After everything I'd done to keep things straight for him at Stager! "This party has nothing to do with me," I said.

"It's Kelsey then, isn't it?"

"What about her?" I asked.

"She's the real reason you dragged me out here, isn't she?"

It was safe to assume Kelsey would be at the wedding—not that I'd have expected him to cancel the whole affair on my account just to spare me from awkward confrontation. Although if he *had* spared me from it, for reasons that made better sense where Cynthia

Ivey was concerned, I wouldn't have blamed him, or minded staying there in that bar all night if necessary as consolation.

Kelsey had known Aaron as well and as long as I had. She'd
inadvertently introduced him to Cynthia, setting off a whole
chain of events, which eventually led to me being there with
him in Allentown, both of us once-divorced and hurtling ourselves back into the fray.

"We're better off now," he said, pulling out the vows he'd
written.

He read them over again and again.

"Oh yes, and soon you'll be telling me that Paul Stager is
a wonderful boss and you want to spend the rest of your life
working there too!"

"I *do* want to spend the rest of my life there," Aaron
explained, rambling on about promotions, having children, and
other opportunities that made even the suds on my lips taste
sour. His situation had devolved toward futility, and it was even
worse than I'd imagined. If my time in sales taught me anything, it was that all of life was a crooked proposition. You get
what you pay for—often less—but I wanted more, and Stager
was destroying the quality of our chicanery. Heaven help him
and Cynthia if that was the kind of future they wanted to spi-
ral downward into together. However restrained I might have
seemed during the nine-to-nine hours, I was not the kind of
man who accepted permanent constriction with great quietus.

In any case, Kelsey had nothing to do with the whole fold
at the time, except that I'd never seen her with another mate

and there was no telling how I'd react if at any point he displayed even the slightest degree of affront or insensitivity.

♦ ♦ ♦

I tried explaining the concept of chivalry for my counselor Marie. "They'd have to tie me to a tree if he'd tried something," I said.

"Are you trying to say you still had feelings for Kelsey?" She asked.

"You've got it all wrong," I answered.

Marie smiled.

She explained now how the conflict in my heart seemed less about the choices I had yet to make and more about all those left irrevocably in the past. But she was wrong. "I'd like to hear more about what happened in Maine," she said.

I was getting there.

I said, "You have to understand, there's a totality of circumstances to take into consideration. I'm not a crazed or hysterical person."

Marie denied ever having thought such a thing, but she didn't have the whole story. Others who knew it had said much worse about me by then.

I said, "It's just important to me that you have the full context, to appreciate the strange interconnectedness of everything, the future irony."

She nodded.

♦ ♦ ♦

At the time of Aaron's wedding, I didn't know what I wanted beyond finding any plausible route out of Stager Auto World. I was searching for ways to fill a void presently occupied by cigarette smoke and alcohol. There was a very real sense growing in me that the questions I'd been asking the universe for years were about to be answered.

"I'm going to be a writer," I told Aaron as he pretended to drink his beer and I guzzled like a pirate on his last day at port.

"You've been saying that for years," he said.

"I'm serious this time," I explained.

"You're never serious," Aaron countered. "And you're never satisfied!"

"What is there to be satisfied with?" I asked him.

I swept up the whole bar in one dramatic motion, with both arms and both half-empty beers outstretched.

"Look at us," I shouted. "We're at the threshold of hell!"

"There's Annie," he whispered. "You just got married five days ago." And then he called me eccentric, paranoid, and delirious.

I told him, "I have been referred to as an ace closer many times—Paul's right-hand man. And do you know why that is? Because I'm dead serious. I'm never satisfied and I understand the principal tenets of human interaction. Who do you think covered your ass?"

"I'm leaving," he said, after considerable time wasted in closed-minded debate. I thought I might let him stew outside, alone with the scavengers who cared even less for his negativity than I did.

"You never listen," I told him. And I'd begun to explain how, on that very same morning, I'd inadvertently discovered one of Annie's old journals whilst rummaging through mysterious boxes stored in the basement.

It was at this time I heard a bottle smash as a fight broke out between two of the bandmates. One accused the other of some offense, and then it spread like wildfire across the barroom as every man took out his pent-up frustrations on the other.

Aaron ran for his pathetic life. Had he stayed to hear the rest about the journal, had he not been such a coward, he might have spared me from the consequence of Maine by talking some sense into me—if he had any sense to give.

I saw him standing by the doorway, which was jammed with fleeing patrons. "Keep your head down, buddy!" I yelled, but it was already too late. He'd gotten caught up in the melee. A man lunged toward him. Perhaps he slipped on the false eyeball, which to the best of my knowledge was still unaccounted for. Aaron raised his hands in defense, one still clutching the vows he wrote. I believe the other hand, clenched in a fist, must have popped the assailant straight in the nose, inciting a full-on riot, which resulted in Aaron getting thrown facedown on the floor and trampled.

"He's the groom!" I shouted, as the revelers cleared and made way for Aaron's scrawny limp body, which I dragged easily with one hand across the smooth wooden boards. Once outside to the safety of the Cadillac, I stretched him out on the backseat and peeled away before anyone called the cops.

I heard him groaning, and he seemed to come to just as we pulled up to the venue, which was already crawling with attendees who were mostly seated near the altar beneath a tremendous willow. "What happened?" he asked.

I told him the whole story. "But we made it out unscathed," I said, though the redness I'd seen over his left eye had swollen and begun to deepen to a shade of purple.

"Oh God, my eye!" He had discovered it.

"Nothing a bit of Tylenol won't fix," I said reassuringly. In his delirium he accused me of being selfish and called me a son of a bitch for trying to ruin his wedding day. He also called into question my account of the preceding events as I scooped a handful of crushed ice out of a fruity concoction I'd purloined on the way out the door. "Quiet down or everyone will hear you," I insisted. Aaron was incensed, beet red, and still bleeding slightly, when a man identified as his father appeared to greet us. I left him in charge, slipped from the wheelhouse, and began a slow steady serpentine to find Annie amidst the waiting congregation.

"Where have you been?" she asked as Aaron's father came charging at us.

Paul was in the seat beside ours, handing out business cards and purging his acumen on anyone who'd listen.

"What in the hell did you do with him?" Aaron's father shouted, pointing his crooked finger at me. I tried to explain everything: how Aaron had gotten carried away and I saved him from an angry mob hell-bent on destruction. The congregation pretended not to notice.

"You're a devil," he began to say, but the violinist suddenly erupted into a frenzied waltz. Aaron and his swollen eye took center stage, waiting along with the rest of us for Cynthia to appear and get on with the proceedings.

"He looks a mess," said Annie. "You're lucky he didn't get you killed, darling."

Then Paul started talking about fidelity again, recounting his days of marriage to a woman who I heard had thrice been driven in shackles to the local sanitarium by his devotions. "Peggy! Oh, Peg! Thirty-five years we shared. And in business! What I wouldn't give to have them all back," he said.

I wondered if she'd have said the same thing if not bridled and badgered into doing so. Cynthia was already halfway down the aisle at this point. She stared toward the altar with great anticipation and a visible mixture of adoration and perplexity. Aaron shrugged as a religious cleric of some sort finally got things underway.

It took us twenty minutes to get through the necessary formalities, and by that time all the parishioners had given up on faithful endurance and developed a ravenous thirst for cajoling and alcohol. I knew everything there was to know about it. When the cleric dismissed us, no one bothered to throw the rice.

One of the more robust attendees approached our herd as we migrated toward free libations and the sound of yesterday's hits playing softly on the veranda. The woman said her name was Tina and claimed we were schoolmates. I said I thought she had me confused with someone else.

"Rob Wildhide," she confirmed with a most heinous and unfamiliar smile.

Aaron's mother stopped by to needle, asking me to apologize. "When it feels right," she whispered, and I agreed because I'd prepared no other speech if called upon to do so as the *de facto* best man.

"That Cadillac sure is a fine automobile, isn't it?" Paul Stager said to Aaron's mom.

She promised Paul that they'd be at the dealership Monday morning to return it, once all the bloodstains were removed from the backseat.

"That sounds fine," said Paul, and I decided to try to keep a low profile for the rest of the evening.

The fat woman who claimed to know me lingered. She appeared twice my age. Had she been one of my teachers?

"Did you hear about Greg?" she asked.

I said I'd never known anyone named Greg.

"Greg Wertz," she replied. She said he overdosed, that his locker was right between ours. And then it all came rushing back from whatever bypass I'd deliberately consigned to oblivion.

I said I was sorry to hear about Greg.

"Isn't it awful?" the woman said.

I think her name was Tori. She then went on to catalogue our other classmates who died in the past twenty years, who all had names I didn't recognize, and shared old stories I had even less regard for than when I apparently lived through them.

I wanted to find Kelsey before she made any more future plans without me in mind—at least for consideration, just in case things in Maine with the treacherous river guides didn't pan out. She was standing by the bar with her new boyfriend, Diego, an abundantly tattooed prison guard from Allentown, by way of Puerto Rico, who was, at that moment, transfixed with his beady eyes set upon me.

Kelsey would have never settled for such a mottled canvas before. She preferred to do her own scarring. She was the type to read romance over mysteries—and I reasoned she must have started off as desperate as I'd become in the days following my marriage to Annie. Now we were both besmirched and still seeking what we lost the day we said good-bye, or something much better.

"Happiness," said a man with rosy cheeks and bloodshot eyes who appeared out of nowhere to stand between us holding up his cocktail. "It's in the ability to love." Annie cocked her head. "The drink," he said. "It's good."

"Yes, I'm sure," I told him. "Tolstoy thought so too, I believe."

He looked at Annie.

"It's a joke," I said, shaking my head. "She's very focused," I explained. "Not sensitive to innuendo. How about it, Annie— should I get us one?"

"Water," she replied.

But I'd forgotten all about her boring request by the time I made it through the seething horde gathered around the bar. Diego was still watching my every move.

I thought someone should have warned Kelsey about prison guards. They're all too familiar with their cages and the only difference between them and the venomous creatures standing on the other side is a bit of shiny aluminum.

"Yes, yes. I understand completely," I heard Kelsey saying to the bartender.

They were discussing the sorry array of drink choices made available, I think.

The bartender smiled, as did I the moment Kelsey turned around and saw me there. She said instantly, "Don't worry, they've got you covered."

I thought she was the only one in the world who could sympathize with my condition, or offer insight regarding the charges I'd uncovered since reading the journal. It was a strange, but rather intoxicating matter of familiarity and contempt. But surely she could help explain what it all meant moving forward.

"It's been a while," I said, as Diego squared off his shoulders like a wild stag with fire in its eyes sizing up a superior bull. I lowered my horns. "Diego," I grunted.

"Well, I just love what they did here," said Kelsey. "How are things with Annie?"

She was standing over by the chocolate fondue, talking with the rosy-cheeked alcoholic and telling him specifics that I had yet to hear about our upcoming trip.

"It's weird," I said.

"For good reason, I'm sure," interjected Diego, who didn't know the first thing about me other than what had been widely circulated in reports of my pursuing strange women over the internet, blackouts, and one exaggerated incident prior to our breakup that involved prescribed narcotics and a loaded .357. It was all hearsay and subject to interpretation.

The revelers closed in. They ate ravenously, like jackals circled around a rotten carcass, bridesmaids bursting out of their silk dresses and howling with laughter as the band played a Bob Seger song.

"Good seeing you," said Kelsey, and I wanted to stop her right then.

I prayed for the words that would help bring a rationale to mixed regret and uncertainty, confessing everything I knew. But nothing rational came to mind, so I smiled like a peasant, and in the morning I was leaving for a lesbian wedding.

I thought of it later—the perfect utterance—when we were out on the dance floor beneath a dawdling silver ball. I was confused, still directionless at the time. But in that moment, Kelsey and I were the only ones there, spinning in the arms of our others, separated by circumstance, sequined gowns, and a chorus ringing in my ears.

Annie asked me, "What's wrong?"

"Nothing," I said. "It's just the wine."

"You've had enough, then."

I told her, "Yes, I do believe I have."

Chapter 3

The next day we were charging ever onward, following a thin strip of uneven pavement not listed on the map, having crossed over into Maine in record time. I was hoping for harmony, and not bloodshed, at the end of the broken road. Annie was elated. She could not stop talking about her friends in Greene, and she drove at breakneck speeds to get there, bypassing tourist destinations and traffic snarls using side roads and detours through the North Woods, then down a five-foot-wide swath of dirt carved into thick brush and over an embankment barely wide enough for her Jeep to fit through.

"Are we there yet?" I asked.

She said, "Almost."

I'd never been to Vacationland, but through thick black forest I could see no sign of anything that resembled the great mountain ranges and rivers that inspired Longfellow and Millay. We went further in, crossed a stream running clear across the lane, and pushed closer to—and farther from—all the wild ideas swirling in my mind. What a jungle! The forest closed in and Annie stopped beside a fallen tree.

The point of this adventure seemed clear enough to me at the time. I'd been waiting to meet Annie's friends. Her past was a subject I'd recently pondered at length, not only because I married her without knowing most of the relevant details, but also because I considered the discovery process a form of catharsis which had, in fact, turned out to be artistically stimulating.

I began taking mental notes when Annie suggested an impromptu hike before things got too hectic for us to spend any quality time alone.

I asked if we should get things started off right. In the back of the Jeep we had a gallon of booze—farm-made wine her father had offered as a gift to the two brides, plus a jar of moonshine Annie knew nothing about. She said no. Annie began rifling through our essentials, tossing aside headlamps and Snickers bars. It was four o'clock, approximately, and she said, "Hurry up, or we're going to miss sunset."

We put on boots and followed a long, lonely path carved between sharp rocks and cinnamon ferns, tracing steps worn down by hikers and probably barefooted natives before them. Annie rarely spoke on long hikes through the woods. She believed in deep, silent meditations, kept a strong pace, and stopped only once that day when we reached a set of cascading waterfalls. I tried asking her if she had any other surprises in store. I was thinking more along the lines of what to expect when we got wherever we were going after finishing the hike.

Annie said all her friends were going to love me and insisted that I love them too.

"What difference does that make?" I asked. I already hated most of them—the one I knew and those I'd read about in graphic detail.

She assumed it was my nerves and leaned in to kiss me. "Just be you," she said.

I assured her from experience that wasn't going to be the best strategy if she wanted me to leave a good impression. My mind was racing. It always was.

"You worry too much," she told me, but I wasn't *concerned*. I was plagued, preoccupied, and half soused most of the time because there was no silencing the demons without alcohol.

It'd taken considerable shrieking to keep me motivated and moving upward in all my un-drunk befuddlement, but she promised the sunset at the peak was a moment not to be missed. And she didn't want to be late for the schedule of activities planned for that evening, either.

Dave Scott lived just over the mountain, a dozen or so miles down the road from where Annie left the Jeep parked along with our provisions. So we continued on, for the sake of time and other important considerations. I abandoned thoughts of confessing exactly how I'd come to know that Dave and other men she kept in close association with had, in fact, once been much more than friends. They might have yet been conspiring, but I was too thirsty for knowledge and moonshine to consider turning back. The whole story had yet to be revealed.

We soon made it to the top and Annie produced the Snickers bars from her pocket—two melted blobs we quickly devoured, licking the wrappers clean. She went to the edge and sat down, letting her long legs dangle over so there was nothing between her muddy boots and the ground below except a thousand feet of gravity. The view was spectacular.

"Isn't it perfect?" she said. And it almost was.

Part of me wanted to leap. But I imagined the smirk on Lee Donegan's pimpled face the moment he heard the news of my demise. I thought of the book I'd never written. And I saw at least a hundred people staring at my corpse at the funeral, with Paul Stager handing out business cards. At least I didn't have to work in the morning.

Annie asked what was on my mind. I told her it was the weight of the universe pressing against me. She laughed, but it was true.

"You were right," she said smiling. "We should have brought the wine."

Annie clearly trusted my instincts, somehow. And she promised never to let propriety, obligation, or good sense get in the way of our drunken doom ever again. To her it was all predestined and written in the stars that'd begun to shine overhead. She said she liked my writing. So I wondered if she might finally be the one to save me from my own propensity for choosing shelter, conscience, and rectitude over divine decree. And I chose from that point onward to write exclusively about her, come what may.

It was all so silly. I laughed and went along with everything she said in the orangish dusk until the sun fell behind the silhouette of a distant mound. Then there were suddenly a thousand shrieking, creeping things that all came to life in the forest like the heathen in Hazard Square who chased their own shadows most Friday nights. To the east, there stretched a vast channel carved into the earth over millennia by swift running waters. Annie said it traced the route to Greene. In the distance we saw the lights of town; it was a good night for setting bearings, talking about dreams, and guessing distances to a great many inestimable points well past the darkening horizon. Annie slid across the flat slab of rock, swearing I'd be a famous writer someday, and we both laid our heads back to view the stars.

"Imagine that," I said.

"What will you write about?" asked Annie, and I said the first thing that came to mind.

"True love," I told her. I began plotting it then, retracing staggered steps in my brain as we both fell silent. I wished I had pen and paper. Then there was a great commotion. "Did you hear that?" I asked.

"It's just the wind picking up," said Annie.

"No. It's coming toward us," I said, and we both sat up, shining light in the direction of what in our imaginings might have been a bull moose or a mass of thick black hair and piercing fangs.

I heard a snap followed by three sharp grunts.

"My God, it's a bear!" exclaimed Annie.

"Where?" said the man who emerged covered in twigs and leafy debris, panting as though one had just chased him.

After we all settled down, he said his name was George Lewis, and that he'd been riding trains for the past three years ever since he lost his dear wife Ellen to cancer. "It feels like it was yesterday," he told us. "But it was a Tuesday, years ago." He pulled a bottle from his drab green overcoat, twisted the cap off, and took a drink.

"I lost my mom around that same time," Annie confided.

"What was it?" asked the man.

"Blood cancer, indirectly," replied Annie as he handed her the bottle. We talked some more and drank a little, but not nearly enough, because it all still hurt so much, directly or indirectly. When he threw the empty jug off the ledge we heard it smash ten seconds later on the rocks below.

"I've got just the thing for this type of heartache back at the Jeep," I told them, but the man insisted he had a train to catch in Lewiston, having missed the sunset that day because of a maze of logging roads that crisscrossed the state of Maine.

He pulled out his pipe, and before long we were all lost in a fog, trying to recount distant memories and struggling to form coherent thoughts. "I always try to find the sun," said George. "It's just gotten hard to watch it go."

He explained he was a manic-depressive, and that he struggled with thoughts of mass casualty and suicide. I thought briefly, *We should watch this man more closely, so as not to get caught up in one of his fits and be thrust over, like rubbish off the rails.* But he was unruffled now, and remarkably kind and poetic for an unabashed lunatic.

I invited him to join us on the trek back down.

"No, no," he said. "You kids enjoy your time together. It'll be Tuesday soon enough."

I knew he was insane, but then, weren't we all? I thanked him for his company and wished him well. "Do you have a flashlight?" I asked.

"Don't need it," said the man. "I've been walking alone through the dark for a very long time."

We said good-bye and left him standing there as we started back through thick brush. We followed the stream, which first emerged as a trickle from the mountainside but grew to over twenty feet wide by the time we'd reached flat ground. We were still talking about George when the trail diverged from the bank, and we took a sharp left to follow the sound of rushing water back toward the trailhead.

Annie thumped along, hopping logs and sloshing through muddy stretches of wetlands, professing her considerations to the bullfrogs and howling back at coyotes whenever they protested. "This *is* bear country," she added, and I kept a watchful lookout, growing more paranoid with each step as my buzz began to wane.

I told her not to slow down.

"We're almost there," said Annie. Soon we were out of breath but upon the Jeep, and I was glad to see it there, not torn apart by hungry predators or ransacked by George or any other lovesick deranged hobo.

Moments later we were back on mottled tarmac, clamoring over potholes and areas where the ancient road returned to silt. Her Jeep rode like a buckboard wagon, but it had good power coming out of the turns and Annie wasn't afraid to use it. I saw the dashboard needle jump each time she straightened out the wheel and leaned heavy on the throttle, trying to outrun malefic thoughts. The dim yellow headlight beams pointed us through a twisted maze of trailer parks and white pine.

She insisted we were getting close, pressed onward, and flogged the tired old engine so that it knocked and pinged louder with each revolution. She had no regard for the posted speed limits or my advice when I told her something was bound to break loose if she kept on pushing.

When it finally did, the force of the explosion rocked us broadside. We skidded on the loose stone until our broken heap came to rest idly by the edge of the road.

"What happened?" asked Annie as a layer of dust settled over the windshield, blotting out the outside world and all the stars overhead.

"You killed it," I said emphatically, knowing we were stranded there until who knows when. We let it sink in.

"I think we should talk," Annie said.

"*Now* what am I supposed to do?"

She said, "First of all, calm down. I think we can make it if we walk the rest of the way. It's not that far. I'm pretty sure it's not."

"The second option?"

"You can stay in the truck beside me tonight and keep me warm and I'll get Dave to fix it tomorrow."

Crickets chirped, and my stinking feet ached and still weren't dry from our last episode. I thought again of George, who'd have probably given anything to spend the night there squabbling beside his bride instead of wandering aimlessly through the wilderness. Annie moved over in the seat, pressed her lips against my cheek, and threw her arms around my neck. We were miles from town and by the dashboard light I could see my breath begin to fog.

"We should turn the battery off," I said, "to conserve power." I checked my phone for service.

"You aren't going to get any signal out here," said Annie. "Why don't you relax?"

She swore she was still feeling high as she appeared to settle in for the overnight, wrapping herself in a blanket. I said it was usually hard to tell with her. She had an offbeat quality when sober, though her positively berserk driving left very little doubt in my mind.

Annie sat back and began flipping through the pages of a worn-out gazetteer. On her breast she still carried her mother's ring. It hung on a gold chain that I never saw parted from her fair skin, where it rolled and sparkled, even in the dark.

"Do you think he jumped?" she asked.

"Who, the transient?"

"I suppose he was."

"No, I think he watched the stars," I said. "He probably smoked a little and said a prayer for—Ellen, wasn't it? He's probably sleeping soundly and dreaming of her right now."

"Maybe."

Annie beat the seat back with the palm of her right hand. She wanted me there to snuggle. I was still trying to process when Annie started speaking about destiny.

Tabitha was the name of her lesbian friend who, in two days, was getting married somewhere farther down the line. "That damned crazy cat," she said, and claimed the whole hobo encounter had been a legitimate signal from the cosmos. "She's always telling me to pay attention to this sort of thing. Things happen for a reason, you know."

She said she completely understood what great purpose there was behind meeting the love-lost man, him winding up there, and our getting stuck along the roadside that night. It had nothing to do with poor judgment.

Before long it was midnight, and Annie didn't let up for one second, talking about happenstance and universality. She explained how in certain circles there was no such thing as coincidence. "Mom died on a Tuesday," she said, as if she had only just realized this as certain other intangibles came into focus. "I've been thinking about how we got married so soon. I've wondered about it sometimes; I've just never said. But if it wasn't the right thing when everything started moving quickly, destiny would've intervened!"

I didn't follow.

"Don't you see? We were meant to be together, Rob, and the past—your past *and* mine—is irrelevant."

At that point the whole cabin shook with the force of her revelation. I hadn't known until then that there was ever a doubt in the poor girl's clearly susceptible mind. "What on Earth are you talking about?" I shouted. "You've been poisoned by a witch!"

"What witch?" she asked perplexedly.

"Tonya!" I replied.

"You mean Tabitha?" she asked.

I said that names were not important. So as not to be distracted by those and other superfluous details, I swiftly moved to deliver my central point with great gusto.

I said, "You can't blame the universe for everything!"

Annie looked at me in shock. She was so beside herself that even the chakras she'd been opening fell momentarily silent as she sprang out from the passenger seat and into the night. I followed her outside to ruminate and get the beer that was buried beneath our cargo in the back.

She was pacing and cursing me for desecrating sacred bonds, speaking in tongues and calling upon me to retract my previous declaration and open my mind to things beyond the reaches of our understanding. I'd begun to suspect she had an undisclosed mental disorder and decided to tiptoe where harbingers were concerned.

I insisted I meant no degree of catastrophic effrontery. Annie paused, and I knew that she'd forgiven my bluntness when she reached into the luggage pile and produced two of the warm beers I'd been rummaging for. We drank them quickly and I soon found it possible to forgive her derangement, but did not turn my back on her, either, until she was passed out in the backseat.

In the interim, we were left deciding what to do to fight the cold. I'd suggested stronger libations, but settled for the plan Annie had in mind as we climbed into the cabin and wrapped ourselves up together in the thin, scratchy wool blanket she seemed to favor. Soon she unzipped my jacket and poured herself over me as if we were teenagers at a drive-in. The great cosmic vale was our theater. We maneuvered like contortionists amidst the jumble of things strewn about in our little nest. Then we both gobbled up every last bit of glut and gratification there was to be had between us until the only thing left on my mind was the potent blackberry port, which she said was never meant for me in the first place.

During the adjournment Annie whispered, "You're the man I've always wanted." But she was already half asleep with her head on my shoulder.

It was only a dream—she was in the insipid gray silence, like the calm before a tremendous storm.

I rarely slept in those days, to keep my most vivid dreams at bay. Some were nightmares—I'd begun having those more regularly.

So I stayed awake. There was no contingency in sight, and, in Maine, nothing else to do but hope for rescue by morning.

Chapter 4

ANNIE TALKED LOUDLY ABOUT A LOT OF THINGS in her sleep, magnificent gibberish about the coming of ages, which I knew was a byproduct of her guilty conscience. That night in the Jeep was no different. She'd grown especially restless by dawn, chuffing and clamoring while the pace of her breathing increased. I thought I should wake her before things got too far out of hand—but then she murmured something about Lee.

There was no doubt in my mind by then that Lee Donegan bedded her one night, alongside the Leigh River in a tent she described in her writing as being "too small for the attitude of his thrusting."

Had it come to her reliving that episode, I'd have quickly interfered.

Their whole romance made me sick, in no small part because she'd denied it while he'd lived with us. She'd accused me of some antediluvian bias when I voiced my suspicions or complained because he was a raft guide. I said the entire concept of a fertile man and a beautiful woman being strictly platonic was a farce; that was the truth.

Now I wondered what else she'd been denying as a matter of curiosity, principle, and possible self-preservation through the course of whatever she was leading me toward. So I let her ramble on.

It was almost morning. I hadn't slept for days in an effort to remain vigilant in the face of perturbation. I tried keeping a positive perspective, but one must never let their guard down in the North Woods. There are a great many monsters there.

One of them scurried down from a tree outside our window with a live cardinal clenched in its fangs. The weasel-like creature stopped to stare at me, unafraid, as I slapped the frosty glass.

I sided with the bird, knowing rightly that everything living in the wild has an insatiable appetite, but what followed was especially grotesque.

Annie was squirming beside me in the seat, panting and about to burst into frenzy, when the rodent made its move. I knew better than to intervene at this juncture. There was no saving the bird. That weasel, I could tell, was prepared to fight tooth and nail for its meal, and could probably rip me to shreds if provoked.

It leapt to the hood, and the sudden *thunk* woke Annie. She opened her eyes to the sight of the varmint dissecting and devouring the carcass just a few feet away. The weasel disappeared moments later, leaving only the cardinal's head in a pool of blood and feathers before Annie even had her bearings back.

"What was that?" she asked.

"Another bad omen," I replied.

She said it made her squeamish. I agreed, and we decided it was best to turn our attention back to the winding road and finding Dave's cabin forthwith.

♦ ♦ ♦

Maine is desolate.

I told Marie that must be why so many twisted freaks lived there, huddled together like rats in tiny secluded nests. My counselor was stoic and, I could tell, searching for the correct clinical index to moderate as I continued on, trying to tell her everything. "Kittery. Portsmouth. Bangor—oh, they're quick to correct, it's *Ban-gor*. What a fucking joke! The whole state is a wasteland with no cell service," I said, squirming in my chair. "I can see why Stephen King likes it so much."

"You have a right to be your feelings," Marie counseled. "But please continue on."

♦ ♦ ♦

Dave Scott emerged from the forest sporting camouflage and lumberjack boots, peering at us through tar-streaked safety goggles as I rolled out of the passenger side door wearing nothing but boxer shorts and sunglasses. His face was bright red from the cold. "Are you guys all right?" he asked. He had spotted the red Jeep through the trees as he was out chopping firewood.

I explained the whole situation while Annie got dressed. Dave stared over my shoulder, assessing damages. Her Jeep was an '01. It had visible rust on all sides and a litany of mechanical problems besides the broken pieces, which hung down from the undercarriage.

"You poor baby," he said as Annie climbed out. "Stuck out here all night long with the animals!"

Meanwhile, everyone was back at the cabin. Dave said Tabitha, her partner, Lynn, Lee Donegan, and a shaman of some kind were already loaded up and asking about us. A mix of other attendees and addicts, half-sloshed at 9:00 a.m., were just starting to arrive. Annie's brother Tom couldn't make it; he'd flown off to Alaska to defile a virginal Inuit girl he met over the internet and said there simply wasn't enough good weed in all of New England to lure him back down from that altitude. They planned a tremendous bonfire that evening in his honor and to celebrate the union, which was the first of its kind in that part of Maine.

We decided to join in after I put on appropriate garb, to make a good first impression, having reached the obvious conclusion that there was nothing to be done with the Jeep.

"So how's old Tommy doing?" asked Dave as he led us through a stand of birches.

"He misses us, I'm sure," said Annie. "And he asked about you and Liv."

Dave said their marriage finally fell apart. It didn't seem to bother him.

"Oh, I'm sorry, I didn't know," Annie replied.

Dave smiled and said, "It's for the best."

His cabin wasn't more than a quarter-mile from the spot where we'd broken down, sitting through the trees beneath a funnel cloud of chimney smoke.

"I told you we were just around the bend!" Annie said to me.

These shanties are littered throughout the North Country, evidence of some attempt at civility in a land where nothing decent thrives.

Dave said, "Welcome home, Annie." The cabin came into view.

All the way there she'd been keeping watch for its bright green front porch swing, which I'd read about in pornographic detail, that set his shack apart from the rest.

There it was fully, the epicenter of an unholy mess, as we walked down the two muddy tracks in the grass that he must have called a driveway. I saw Lee Donegan dry humping the poor, sick girl standing beside him. She feigned abhorrence as he thrust his hips against her to the rhythm of someone drumming inside.

"Annie Cotner!" he exclaimed, temporarily relieving this girl from her commission.

"It's Wildhide now," said Annie.

"Well, you'll always be Cotner to me," Lee said, and I thought, just for being an indignant asshole, I might strangle him by his thin neck before the whole thing was even started.

But it wasn't the right time, and, as I said, I wanted to make a good impression. Besides that, there were more than twenty people in the immediate vicinity who, at that state in the proceedings, would have called me brash for squashing him at first sight, having not had the proper introduction to our sordid history. Dave said it was time for breakfast.

Tabitha was in the kitchen making *ding-ding*, something she bragged was inspired by a trip to South India. I was trying to unknot and assimilate, as rafters do, by gargling with the local swill wherever I could find it. "Rob, this is Tab," Annie said.

"Oh yes, yes—it's very nice to meet you," I replied, setting my drink aside for proper introductions. Her partner, Lynn, was there too.

"I've heard so much about you," Tabitha said.

Instead of shaking hands, she clapped hers together three times and handed me a piece of what appeared to be some kind of jerky. I thought cows were sacred in India, but her partner assured me there was nothing sacred there or anywhere else.

Annie said Tab had *au fait* worldviews, and *subtle perception* as a result of travels incommunicado from Lynn, who'd stayed on top of the supposedly transcendental journey through Facebook over the three seasons it took for Tabitha to become enlightened. "We want to hear all about it," Annie said, and then it seemed up to everyone not swapping river stories to walk around listening like disciples, slack-jawed and pretending to like the taste of tree bark because we'd never been to Zanzibar.

Tabitha chattered like one of Dirk's cockerels about Thailand and Portugal, saying she'd hitchhiked across the country and finished writing her memoirs while working for room and board at a sweat lodge in Arizona. That's where she found Ted Ford, the officiant and all-time master of ceremonies, whom she'd encountered as he rolled in the sand outside of a hut out west, in a peyote- and temperature-induced haze. He'd professed to be in constant communication with spirits. "*Coo De Khaa,*" she'd heard him say.

"Do they see me?" Tabitha had asked him.

"Yes, they do," he had replied, claiming they were calling her to be one with love, a message Tabitha must have had to interpret. She'd then joined him in the cool, soft sand, naked beneath the desert stars, and whenever the spirits moved them they filled their cups with drink and smoked some more until the sun came up and all the visions were clear.

"Lynn and I are kindred," she said now, explaining how she'd come back to Maine to reconnect, following the advice of oracles and believing in stars and other things beyond the reach of any sane rationale.

Evidently Lynn became distant while Tabitha was gone as a way of coping with the stress of the two jobs she worked to pay Tabitha's credit card bills. This was the consequence of a lack of her own reasons to be high and reckless in the name of illumination.

"It's rare to have that level of commitment outside the community," Annie proclaimed, because none of the men she'd tried to love ever cared so much for her while she was off on her own weird, wild trips.

I tried to say being gay had nothing to do with it, but couldn't get a word in edgewise.

"Yes, men are pigs!" shouted Tabitha.

Ted was in the living room, trying to get some pretty little thing drunk. "Damn, Tab," he said. "This is unfair!"

"Well, it's true," she told him. "But most of us don't hold it against you."

Outside on the veranda, Lee and Dave were getting stoned along with the patriotic contingent. I went out with my cocktail to soak it all in. I breathed deeply before joining the group on tattered lawn chairs. They were pointing their revolvers at a row of plastic jugs. They quickly established that the jugs had a tremendous likeness to a human skull when contacted by a hollow-point.

"It's a damn *A-rab*," Dave said as he squeezed off the first round.

It cracked from the tip of his barrel in a puff of smoke but sailed wide of its target, striking an empty drum instead, as the rest of the Iraqi death squad commenced with open fire. "Go ahead, try it," Dave offered a short while later, insisting it was much harder than it looked.

More than half the jugs were still intact when I snatched the weapon up and fired without hesitation, watching as one of the illustrative heads exploded on impact. "Now do that standing up," Dave said. I repeated the feat once again, this time striking the target low on the rail, causing the bullet to ricochet. Fragments went in every direction, also hitting the two adjacent jugs.

"*Woo hoo!*" I shouted.

Then I heard someone exclaim, "My eye! I lost my eye!"

"The son of a bitch shot Lee," another man yelled. Lee ejected from his chair in a fit of dismay with one hand covering the blemish and the other still instinctively clutching a beer.

Then Lee charged me, right as the others came rushing out to investigate the commotion, including Annie and the entire bridal party.

"Hold on a minute," Dave shouted, grabbing Lee by the collar in an effort to render aid. "Now, let me get a look at you . . . hold still!"

Lee shrieked, "I'm blind!" as the crowd gathered to gawk.

"You've got your eye closed, you damned fool," Dave said. "And it ain't nothing but a nip on the cheek!"

Moments later, Lee was driving himself to a clinic in Greene for stitches, having not found anyone at the party sympathetic or sober enough to take him. Dave stayed behind to keep a close eye on me.

In the backyard, adjacent to the shooting gallery, there was a range of other amusements to keep me occupied during intermission, including a keg of beer and what appeared to be an in-ground hot tub.

Now, I'd stayed at some of the finest resorts in southern New Jersey that Paul Stager's money could afford in the pursuit of industry and better closing ratios. Many of those fine establishments featured hot tubs and furnished alcohol for free. I'd once had to recuse myself from duty, citing influenza, when in reality, I was severely dehydrated as a result of marinating for hours, drunk, spouting mad stories to anyone who'd listen. It was Stager's fault for putting someone with my particular weakness for indulgence in that position to begin with. But never had I seen a tub ostensibly buried in the dirt of virgin wilderness. A garden hose and orange extension cord stretched across the courtyard toward the irresistible steam that poured from beneath the lid.

I called upon Annie to accompany me as I stripped down to boxer shorts. One of the lesbians joined in and helped me remove the cracked and faded top, which she propped against a row of chicken wire for privacy. Annie was talking with Dave and was, at that point, evidently too preoccupied with him to have noticed my amazing discovery.

The lesbian went in first, au natural. I wasn't sure whether it was Tabitha or Lynn, because they looked entirely like twins when fully cloaked in matching flannel. Then, when the other one came out of the cabin teasing her mate for having a secret obsession with dick, I knew that it was Lynn who, seconds later, was sitting with me in the warmth of the foamy, oscillating water.

I have always been a faithful man, and moreover would not have fraternized in any condition with a naked lesbian with Annie close-by. It was not, in my mind, a plausible sexual encounter. Nevertheless, Lynn made eyes at me in broad daylight. Dave's Guinea hens were pecking close by, watching while she tried communicating her intentions telepathically. The heat was almost unbearable, and it intensified the intoxicants coursing through our veins.

Lynn must have assumed I didn't receive her message of carnal intent, because I felt her foot touch mine and hairy legs move up and down my shins to the rhythm of the incessant drumming. It was an awe-inspiring experience, of which I took mental note.

Before long, she pounced like a wild dog hungry for meat. I pushed her back, swearing it was fever, causing a great splashing tidal commotion, which resulted in us becoming entwined. I was gasping for air as she dragged me under when the others descended upon us, accusing *me* of malicious intent!

I crawled out in my underwear, insisting it could all be explained—but I didn't know how.

Tabitha was beside herself, having jumped to certain conclusions along with the rest of them. One member of the congregation snagged an oar and threatened to bash me with it. It was pandemonium, and I believed that I was about to be overrun. Annie was even shouting obscenities by then, and did nothing whatsoever to defend my character against baseless attack.

"She's gay!" I declared in my own defense.

Then Tabitha swiped the oar from the hands of one of them, claiming I'd tried to "turn" Lynn—a day ahead of their wedding, no less! Before I could say that I didn't even know that was possible, she raised the paddle over her head.

I waited for the blow when, at last, Lynn proclaimed that she'd slipped and cut her foot on a piece of broken glass that was submerged beneath the froth. She produced the shattered piece, remarkably, to the marvel of everyone—especially myself—and Tabitha lowered her weapon.

After that, Lynn called upon Ted Ford to restore positive mojo, which he said required shamanic healing, the holding of hands, and more pot—especially where her partner was concerned. We worked to restore balance with pistols holstered, chanting ourselves into oblivion.

They performed a singing ritual, then, and the women danced like pixies around a bonfire well into the night, long after I'd given up on restorative powers.

I went inside to sulk in peace and scribble my scattered thoughts on scrap paper I found while foraging through Dave's cabin. The words, as usual, did not come easily.

Lee returned sometime after ten o'clock wearing an eye patch. He was tripping over himself from a lack of depth perception and the pain meds he was on, claiming Lou Reed was dead. "Rest in peace," he said, and sat down at the table as I had, with a drink in each hand and a clear intention of going until all that was left of our booze and good sense was gone.

It didn't take long.

Soon it was just us two. Annie and the other lunatics had put away amulets and wooden sticks to sleep side-by-side on the floor like cultists, alongside decaying animal furs and wet boots. I'd said I was too moved by their performance to sleep, but it was only that Lee had found another bottle: moonshine, this time, from the back of the Jeep. The Jeep that I noticed Dave had put on cinderblock stilts.

Under the circumstances, Lee seemed as good as anyone else there to drink it with. He put on some good music for us to listen to.

"Oh, this is the *shit*!" he said, focusing his good eye, which was dark and glassy, on the stereo system. Then he jumped back, swaying to the familiar sound of clanging electric guitars that thankfully drowned out the sounds coming from the next room and the static hum of ideas swirling inside my head.

He promised the best was yet to come. I didn't ask what he meant; I didn't even want to know, so long as it didn't involve me. I decided that it wouldn't, if I could avoid it. The minute Dave got Annie's Jeep put back together, I'd be gone, with or without Annie.

She could have vouched for me, at least. But it was clear enough, in my drunkenness, where she'd chosen to tether her musty devotions.

I'd known men similar to those beasts of the north, and cursed the stars every time one of them pulled onto the car lot with a petrified turkey's foot dangling from his rearview. But raft guides are a special hybrid breed. Not just indignant hard-asses with red necks and a penchant for trophymanship; not hippies either. Beatniks are far more amiable, but Annie couldn't stand patchouli. She preferred pine tar.

How she fell for me was a mystery. Or was it a maneuver? There was no telling, with the state that I was in.

Dave came through, spooking around once more before going to bed. He said we'd go into town for parts in the morning, depending upon his disposition. "There's a wedding to consider," he added.

Lee was really going now. He popped another one of his pain pills and grabbed up Tabitha's bongo.

"Cut this shit out," Dave insisted. "We're all trying to sleep."

"Fuck you, Dave," said Lee, cranking the music louder each time he was asked not to until finally Dave had enough and wrestled him over the djembe until both Lee and the wooden goblet were thoroughly and completely smashed on the living room floor. Dave turned the music off and Lee went outside to sulk and smoke weed, singing "Sweet Jane" at the top of his lungs until he ran out of contentious energy.

I was sitting in my chair half frozen, breathing in wood smoke and the stench of my own booze-rotten breath. It was almost dawn. Everything was quiet except for the retching of the afflicted writhing in the next room. These were not my kind. I didn't know where I belonged or what I was supposed to do when I got there, so I waited for a clearer sign and hoped, by tomorrow, there'd at least be transportation.

Chapter 5

THE UNIVERSE HAD OTHER PLANS. There is no quick explanation. It could have been the moonshine, but when I closed my eyes to stop the room from spinning, my mind skipped straight to dreaming. I'm not a diviner, but I saw the forecast.

It was New Year's Day last year, the day many knots tied with Kelsey came apart and I began to give up on thinking we could stop the sudden free-fall from rapture to perdition. I was standing on the corner of Spring Street and Maple at 3:00 a.m., waiting for her in dreamy darkness amongst the many wasted dirges as they shuffled home like frenetic zombies from the bars downtown. She almost made it home from dinner, a special all-you-can-eat—or drink—buffet without puking in one of the neighbor's shrubs. Now she blamed cocktail shrimp for her gagging.

"They forgot to bomb us again this year," said an old man in festive American garb who stumbled up to me with a bottle in his hand. He asked me to hold it so he could relieve himself on a lamppost at the end of our drive. I told him he'd better watch out.

"There's cops crawling all over this place," I said.

"Treasonous swine," the man sniped, taking back his tonic. He thought the government was responsible for the attack on 9/11, and challenged anyone within earshot who thought otherwise to a battle of wits or fists. "I'm a sovereign citizen," he declared, and I watched him march around, to the delight of the passing horde, in a peerless display of rebellion. He burned down the alleyways, tossing around wild accusations until the deputy sheriff arrived with a savage barking dog at his side and forced him to surrender or be masticated.

"Give me liberty or give me death," I heard the reveler exclaim as he was promptly shackled, dragged, and then stuffed into a waiting patrol car, party hat and all, with no further ado.

"Where are they taking him?" Kelsey asked, having mended just in time to witness this.

"The nut house," I told her. "And they're probably going to flog and feather him until his brain is like Jell-O."

Kelsey assured me that I was destined to end up there, too. She said if I kept drinking at this pace and working such long hours at the dealership, she'd have to visit me at the state hospital in Danville.

"Would you visit?" I asked her.

"Of course I would," she said. "I'm sure they've got drugs strong enough to make you rational, at least during visiting hours."

She was obviously feeling much better. I told her I was perfectly lucid when I'd explained, moments earlier, that I had work in the morning and therefore could not agree to any impromptu retreat to the Adirondacks.

As a tenet of her desire to have lots and lots of children, I agreed long ago to maintain gainful employment at the car dealership in exchange for her overlooking certain eccentricities involving copious amounts of alcohol. It was all for the sake of better writing, liberating the creative mojo that I suppressed and, by extension, feeding the mouths of many hungry hypothetical kids.

"It requires a level of dedication," I said.

Kelsey knew exactly what and whom I was speaking of—the future little Marshall, Margaret, and Tom—when I insisted that Paul Stager would fire me at the drop of a hat if I didn't show up to oversee his Holiday Extravaganza. God knew Aaron couldn't do it on his own, and the rush of patrons, hungry for good honest deals and hot dogs, would overwhelm him.

"You work too much," Kelsey replied.

I said, "The vultures will eat him alive."

Perhaps, had it not been for the fact that her wanton maternal ambitions included no other provision for fiscal accommodation other than my own personal sacrifice on *their* behalf, I might have agreed to her plan for reckless ascent into the mountains. But someone had to be the responsible custodian of our future, even if I was totally plastered.

By then, Kelsey was shitfaced too. That was the only condition in which she'd ever suggested blowing off work for the sake of any form of rehabilitation—or *anything*. I don't know why, but the weight of consequence made her crazy, even when it might've resulted in renewal.

I tried telling her that she should drink more often.

Then she sobered up.

Suddenly it was her high-pitched, shrieking voice in odious soprano that all the neighbors heard. One of them shouted his dismay from the bedroom window as we negotiated the terms of our increasingly tenuous arrangement.

Kelsey said if I wasn't man enough to stand up to the insidious Paul Stager and spend New Year's with her instead of the suckers, she'd find someone else more suited to the task. I thought that it was just a ruse, an alcohol-induced contrivance to see if I was committed to the cause.

So in the dark I proclaimed that I loved her before God, nature, and all other things. Even the revelers on Spring Street heard my declaration and swayed, clear of entanglement, to the opposing sidewalk.

"Shut the fuck up!" shouted our neighbor.

"He's used to this," I assured Kelsey, whispering, in an effort to spare him and everyone, including myself, from her ire, which threatened to destroy the optimism of the holiday affair.

She said she had her heart set on the mountains.

I reminded her that her heart was set on a lot of things, most of which were never possible to attain simultaneously without one consuming the other, or me, in the pursuit. I didn't disapprove. It was her ravenous appetite for everything at once that first drew me to her, and kept me there for a long while like a moth attracted to flame.

"You think too much," she replied, adding that I always chose work over her, and then proceeded to outline her laundry list of grievances.

I took it into consideration, but assured Kelsey, in any case, that slogging through thick primordial muck in the wilderness would offer no respite.

I went north with Aaron just few weeks prior. We both swore it'd be the last time. My thighs were still chafed. He was beside himself with distress, and altitude had only exacerbated the strain.

There was no consoling him. I should have known better than to take him bushwhacking. So I told her the mountains were no place for the afflicted.

"That Paul Stager is a merciless son of a bitch for keeping you there late again," I'd said to Aaron as we were struggling at five thousand feet. "On your birthday no less!"

It was steep, unpleasant terrain, made more horrid by the smell of earthly decay and the knowledge that we were there gasping it in by choice.

It must have been the rage that kept him trekking onward, upwards, in spite of my numerous attempts to negotiate a compromise. He stayed silent for the longest time.

I suggested we pause at the next promontory to take in the view, and then head back to Albany for late night rabble-rousing with the locals. We'd stopped there at a corner bar for provisions on our way. They were all in good spirits, and the feeling rubbed off, but didn't last long enough to sustain us for the journey.

Aaron seemed especially depleted and in need of restoration as we climbed. But we were miles from anywhere and anyone, now stomping in the dark by lamplight, having underestimated the topography and the time it would take to get there.

I knew he had a lot on his mind.

Aaron had planned to stay the night at our house after his wife directly accused him of infidelity, a condition she'd inaccurately correlated to his erratic work schedule. Kelsey, instead of consoling the poor man, was quick to needle, pointing out that the evidence skewed against him cast a broad shadow on me, as well. After that, the whole thing erupted and might've devolved more quickly had I not suggested we leave in search of higher ground.

I'd never even heard of Cynthia Ivey. Aaron never mentioned her until we reached a rocky precipice halfway up the mountain, where we saw a tremendous lake outstretched below, reflecting the moonlight from above.

"All people are monsters," I said.

"They're not all bad," Aaron replied.

I told him, "No! Have you lost your mind? Don't you remember the Catholic priest who tried to screw us for a nickel?"

He said, "He worked with orphans."

"Ha! I'll bet he did!"

Aaron acknowledged my finely tuned sense of intuition, which made me a formidable adversary at the negotiating table, but accused me of harboring bitterness also. He set his pack down on the flat rock and produced a flask he'd wisely kept hidden in reserve until conditions warranted.

We were both thirsty and aching from the shoulders down, so I warmly congratulated him for his preparedness—a sudden aptitude in the venue of wilderness survival. Then we drank until whatever it was had gone. He finished it, mostly, and screwed the top back on.

"Got any more surprises?" I asked him eagerly.

Aaron nodded and I wondered what he might procure from his magic bag of treats next. Snickers bars?

He said he was thinking about his wife and felt awful for leaving her at home.

"That horrible nag?" I replied.

"We're the horrible ones," he said, now standing at the edge.

I thought for sure he was about to jump. If you'd seen his face in the lamplight, squinted and twisting in agony over matters I didn't fully understand, you'd have lunged for him too.

In an effort to spare him from apathy and save him from his own self, I wrapped my arms around his skinny, emasculated trunk, trying to wrestle with the gloom. I dragged him slowly to where I could better keep control the situation. He fought me the whole way down and began flailing at the last second, as I'd nearly had him pinned. We were still dangerously close to going over when he tried beating me away with his fists. In the midst of this, I assured him that everyone thinks about it.

"But you can't give in to the darkness!" I shouted.

Aaron wasn't listening and shrieked the moment I heard something snap, which turned out to be his left arm.

"Goddamn it!" he wailed.

"It's for your own good," I said, instantly releasing my hold.

It took a while for him to calm down after that.

He eventually maneuvered his frail appendage back into position. I encouraged him, saying that we were all dislocated in one way or another, though it seemed to offer no solace as I heard the limb pop back into place. He shrieked yet again, but it was clear that through the intervention he'd regained his will to live.

As we slid ourselves away from the ledge, he cursed me and said that when we got back, a lot of things were going to change.

For one, we were never going hiking again. I recommended he stay clear of any high rooftops, also, until he got his head screwed back on straight.

"I wasn't going to kill myself, you crazy bastard!" he exclaimed.

He then told me he'd taken a mistress and planned on moving in with her. The situation was complicated, of course, but it all circled back around to the desperate measures he'd resorted to as a good man in his bad hours. Cynthia Ivey represented a broad new beginning. I understood that part completely, even though I had never been unfaithful to Kelsey.

Kelsey would have agreed with Aaron completely when he claimed that I was a bad influence, prone to wild exaggeration of fact, in spite of my best intentions. I denied this in totality, even before he airily murmured it underneath his breath as we were coming off the mountain.

♦ ♦ ♦

That New Year's Day, in the early morning hours, Kelsey eventually agreed to drop the Adirondack thing. I swore to my credibility once more, saying that if I was going to have to endure her irreconcilable bickering all the way there, up the trail and on the mountain, then I'd throw myself off when we reached the top.

A few hours later, Aaron and I were on the lot, having abandoned resolutions as the festivities got underway. He was roasting hot dogs at ten o'clock in the morning in the shadow of a twenty-foot inflated sky-dancing mannequin. It was maybe thirty-five degrees, and the buzzards were already circling. The early birds shuffled in. Those were an unscrupulous bunch of elderly fowl who complained a lot and never bought anything. There is no hyperborean condition that could separate salesmen from their quarry, or prey from the scent of free meat wafting down the street.

Aaron hadn't moved in with Cynthia. At that point the angst over having to break it to his poor pathetic wife was too much to bear, so he'd taken the high road, instead convincing Caroline that she was amiss and foolish for doubting his virtue—at least until he built up the nerve to confess to her and everyone.

Paul emerged to circulate, sidle, and ensure the occasion was a profitable one. This was enterprise at its finest.

Aaron knew Paul would disapprove of his extra-curricular activity, and for reasons I could not understand, gave more credence, in his private declarations, to potential fallout at Stager than the prospect of his soon-to-be ex-wife murdering him in his sleep.

Aaron's wife was a fierce, hateful woman with a mouth like an air raid siren—at least as it pertained to me. She had no sense of humor. I kept in limited contact, avoiding vexatious persons generally, but also because she'd long ago banished me from their property in retaliation for my having said some off-color thing that'd been misinterpreted.

Now she was standing at the front of the line behind the grill, and seemed to have no trouble granting pardon in exchange for the first foot-long I handed her. Aaron had instructed me to be civil toward Caroline, which I always had been, and to use the utmost discretion as it pertained to his indiscriminate libido.

I'd told him that I pitied the poor woman, which he recognized was saying something given my propensity for harboring ill will in perpetuity toward those I felt had abused me. But this two-timing charade was overkill, and I wasn't about to become complicit without going on the record as saying so. Aaron noted it, and said she'd find someone better than him once he finally got the balls to come clean. A fetishist, perhaps?

But even a masochist would've been intimidated by the site of her there, plowing through Paul's hot dogs at an unprecedented rate, bitching about the condiments or lack thereof while the others waited and bristled in line behind her. They were revolted. She chastised Aaron for not rebuking them as they forcibly matriculated to the sides of the grilling station demanding service.

"How 'bout a test drive?" Paul asked the patrons. He tried handing one a business card.

"We want hot dogs!" the man barked.

Caroline had six by the time I stopped counting. Before the extravaganza turned toward rebellion, I decided to procure a second barbeque from storage to try and keep pace with supply and demand.

That's when I turned up our first legitimate customer of the day, a chew-spitting hillbilly who rolled up with the window open to ambush me on my way inside. He kicked off negotiations before he even stepped out of the truck.

I said, "Welcome to Stager."

"Now let me stop you right there," he replied. He opened his door and proceeded to outline a regular distrust and disdain for car salesmen, followed by a list of demands.

I'd heard it all before, insipid drivel too banal, pathetic, and clichéd to glorify. I blocked it out, cut right to the chase, and minutes later the hillbilly and I were cruising. He'd wanted to test drive a Silverado, so we took the normal loop on the freeway. I could tell he was a buyer. He had his trade title in hand and a blank check in his shirt pocket.

Paul would've been thrilled, except things got off track at about the halfway point just outside of Hazard. I received an important call from the receptionist. She said it was urgent. The hospital had called saying Kelsey had an episode. It was a bad one. I wasn't sure how bad.

I encouraged the hillbilly to change course. There wasn't time for debate.

"Let me drive, goddamn it!" I said.

He refused, and so when he continued heading away from the clinic and toward the dealership, I had no other choice but to kick the truck out of gear and threaten to knock his jaw loose if he didn't pull over. When he eventually did, I fought him over control of the driver's side door handle and then pried the man out of the cockpit and left him standing in the street as I sped toward the hospital.

When I got there, it was a melee of confusion. No doctors in sight, only nurses and orderlies trying to answer questions for the throngs of stricken and bereaved strangers who filled the tiny emergency room.

"Can you tell me—where is Kelsey Wildhide?" I asked an attendee over the shoulder of one of the afflicted.

"You'll have to wait your turn, sir," she replied.

I waited for a half hour in line before returning to the desk and politely asking the same question. At that point the burly man who'd occupied her attention from the time I ran in said "Wait your turn or I'll sock you, buddy!"

Now, I am not a violent person by default, but this pushed me over the edge.

I told him, "I will not be threatened or harassed by you, you indignant scum!" At which point he made good on his previous assertion and knocked me out cold on the waiting room floor.

The last thing I remembered thinking was, if he tried something I'd put him into the same hold I used on Aaron, and break his arm like a toothpick. But the man was a serious contender with a short temper and a strong right hook, so I never got the chance.

When I came to, there was a doctor hovering over the bed. "You need to relax," he said. "This should help with the pain."

"What are you giving me—Quaaludes?"

Here was a balding shrew with an advanced scientific degree trying to pump me full of tranquilizers like a common pusher, when all I'd wanted was to find my wife.

"You listen here," I told him. "I want answers! I have a right to know what's going on!"

"How dare you speak to me in that belligerent tone!" he said.

It was fine with me if the man had a God complex, and most doctors do, but it was only Kelsey I was thinking of when I then took extraneous measures, threatening to give him good reason to come down from his perch and start cooperating. "You better wise up, man," I said, "Or I'll have you wrapped up and chained in bed with those pestilent slobs you've been lying to in here!"

"I could have you thrown into a sanitarium!" he replied.

And that may very well have been the truth, but I told him I was only going to ask once more.

He stared deeply into my eyes and saw that I was serious. Convinced of my strong propensity for rage-fueled improvisation when faced with trouble, he pointed down the hall. "Past the elevators—and don't come back!" he shouted.

I stumbled away in half a daze from the Quaaludes, and found the name Wildhide amidst others scribbled on a whiteboard that hung outside a series of examination rooms. Inside I saw a flurry of activity, a mural depicting rainbows and crippled children playing in the sun, and what appeared to be a dead body in repose on a gurney beneath a sheet. What had these evil quacks done with her?

"We'll get to you in a moment," said a nurse who saw me pushing against the locked doors, covered in blood which continued to leak from my lip and dripped down onto my light-blue Stager jacket. I told her I was fine.

"Kelsey Wildhide?" I asked for the tenth time. She was the one in need of doctoring.

The nurse attendant only shrugged.

I decided if the loathsome sawbones had harmed her in any way practicing rogue medicine, there'd be hell.

Kelsey was stricken with some sort of rare psychogenesis, a chronic short-circuit almost no one knew about besides me. It was not only alcohol-induced, but also exacerbated by factors such as anxiety and sleeplessness.

I blamed myself for keeping her up late the night before.

Thank God we weren't in the mountains, I thought. Otherwise there'd be hillbillies poring through symptoms on WebMD, trying to figure things out.

"Let me in!" I demanded, bypassing the nurse altogether.

For the sake of expediency, I tried hurtling myself through the blockade without warning or waiting for clearances. I had a running start at the doors and expected them to fall easily on my first attempt at crashing them. They didn't. The nurse didn't seem surprised, but I was seeing stars.

Through a single pane of thick institutional glass, I saw the doctors conspiring and scratching their blue bonnets, trying to figure what to do with me next. "Do you think I can't see you? Do you think I won't eventually knock these doors down?"

Soon, one of them came rushing over to explain from the other side of the glass. I had to read his lips. "We're running more tests," he said.

They sent out a man who I assumed was an orderly because of his calm demeanor.

He emerged from the other side, motioning with one finger for me to hold. I gave him the benefit of the doubt, ignoring the rush of adrenaline and impulse. I saw the door slowly closing. There was a moment there where I could have taken advantage of the opportunity, before it latched, to streak past in a blaze of glory. But I didn't. He checked in with the nurse, who suddenly seemed bewildered. They huddled together for a while behind the desk, whispering, probably hovering a finger over the call button for security in case I freaked. Had they never seen a concerned husband before?

Then I saw the man sign a document. It must have been an admissions form of some kind. He reeked of marijuana as he approached; I reasoned that he had been out back, smoking up on break, when they called him in to keep me occupied. He still had stems stuck to his black silk jacket. It said *Mountain Chief* on the front, and I thought I must be dreaming. I was too distraught to put it all together. He seemed to know the condition, so I let him apprise me without further speculation—but I could tell he was hiding something.

"She had an episode," he informed me. That wasn't the whole story.

Then he apologized.

"For what?" I asked.

He said, "The whole situation." Which didn't explain anything.

I wanted straight answers, so I assured him that I'd eventually uncover the whole truth about what was going on behind closed doors. "And I'll turn this whole place into a mortuary, if necessary!" I said.

"Oh, there's no need for that!" he replied as his eyes met mine for the first time since he'd started beating around the bush. Now we were getting somewhere.

He said everything was well under control and promised Kelsey would be out in short order.

"She *is* going to live?" I asked him.

He said *yes* without hesitation, because he'd seen this kind of thing many times before.

"Are you some sort of doctor?" I asked.

"Oh, I'm not a doctor," he answered, but cited other specialized training he had in that regard. He assured me he'd dealt with emergencies before. "You *can* trust me on that—I'm a certified raft guide."

Chapter 6

THERE ARE THINGS I REMEMBER and things I forget about my time in Maine. I've tried hard not to remember some of it, and tried harder not to fill in too many blank spaces with dark imaginings and conjecture, even for the sake of therapy. There comes a point when even the disillusioned must keep moving on or risk being swallowed by the fog.

"Permanent affliction was a real danger here," I told Marie.

"I think you were doing okay, all things considered," she said. "Are you still having the dreams?"

"They're visions."

"Visions. You're still having those?"

"Yes, I am."

"And you think they mean something, especially?"

"Of course I do."

It was clear by her puzzled look that we were wading into strange and unfamiliar clinical waters. It was about to get deeper.

Yes, it takes time to recover from significant trauma and clear the head, but I had serious real-life decisions to make. It was her job to help me, for God's sake. If I thought there was time for proper rehabilitation, I'd have found another, better-trained psychiatrist, who was more open-minded and suited to the task.

I'd rehashed it all at least a hundred times in my mind when Marie asked me to continue on, citing multiple unresolved issues leading up to my moment of crisis. She said feelings of fear, bitterness, and anger were all a normal part of the healing process, but I was tormented and tripping dangerously close to the edge. And there was no coming back after that.

◆ ◆ ◆

I didn't know what time of night it was when Annie's so-called friends in Maine called me out, or why the door was locked. They tried forcing their way into the cedar plank room where I was sitting on the couch next to another man who claimed to be the limo driver. He said his name was Guy Manchetti and that he'd been through quite an ordeal.

"I knew I never should have taken this job," he moaned, and then crept wearily across the creaking floorboards to peer through thin slats covering a window.

"What are we looking for?" I asked him.

"My limousine," he replied.

The last thing I remembered was drinking moonshine with Lee Donegan. The chorus he sang still played over and over in my delirium, just like the soundtrack of a far-out movie, except it was all some form of real life. This could have explained the headache and dizziness, but not the man in loafers now shuffling on all fours, flashlight in hand, to get a look beneath the locked bedroom door.

He said they'd tried to poison him with roofies that night, after the ceremony, and then drove off with his car—an '89 Lincoln with all new upholstery.

"Ceremony?" I repeated back to him.

"That's right," he replied. That's when I knew an entire day had passed without my cooperation.

Guy said the drugs didn't take, so he'd given chase and commenced with clobbering the one he held responsible for the infraction, a miserable Paul-Bunyan-looking dufus who'd slipped away only to return moments later with reinforcements wielding paddles. By that time, the limo driver said he was feeling pretty woozy. The floories set in; otherwise he'd have smashed the lot of them with his two oversized Italian fists. Instead he'd had to make a run for it and had holed himself up in the same room where I'd been laid out comatose on the couch.

"I thought you were dead!" he exclaimed. "Who are these evil mothers?"

"They're seasoned raft guides," I told him.

He nodded and claimed he'd never heard of such a thing. It's not a legitimate profession. Then he recounted in detail the rest of what I missed. Guy said that the brides exchanged dildos instead of wedding rings as a shirtless officiant chanted Native American spirituals. They gave out potion for the toast, which he sipped, following decorum, though it tasted like pond water.

"I *knew* something was wrong," he said. "This one kept eyeing me. He was asking for my keys."

The others drank in vast quantities from that point on—and had apparently now teamed up and resorted to pounding on the bedroom door, cutting Guy's story short. They tried to slip credit cards and other clever implements between the latch, but it was bolted from the inside. "We're not going anywhere," I heard one of them saying.

"Joyriding SOBs," Guy shouted back. "Neither are we!"

He believed that his beloved chariot had been made a roving hotbox, and was flogged and battered to pieces, a desiccated husk of its once imperial self. The thought of it drove him to conniption. Naturally, he wanted retribution. The man had endured profound harassment while prostrated to these river dirtbags in pressed formalwear, which was now tattered and ripped, bearing signs of the encounter. I told him I was sympathetic.

"Yes, of course you are—just look at you," he said. "We have to set our course and get out of here!"

It was at this point I began to seriously consider abjuring: leaving Annie—not only there in the North Country, but for good—and not looking back until Guy Manchetti had me sequestered permanently across state lines. This is what Maine does to you. I was frenetic, presenting signs of hysteria, and was telling all about Kelsey, Annie, and her journal, when the banshees came calling once again.

"We need to play it cool," I told the limo driver.

He was wrapping his fist in bed linens and dispensing his plans for offense and wanton aggression. He said he kept a loaded revolver in the hideaway tucked above the rear wheel.

"They're those wire-rimmed jobs," he added, vowing to come back with a pipe bomb if the raft guides had ruined those or the Austrian crystal service set, which he claimed had once been used by Johnny Depp.

"Let's be reasonable," I told him. "They might be river rats, but I can negotiate with these animals!"

But Guy wanted nothing to do with arbitration. The SOBs started this feculence, and now he was going to rub their noses in it.

So I crawled out the window before Guy slipped his moorings, and found myself back on two legs trying to act natural as I passed through a courtyard filled with half-baked campers returning from the wedding ritual. Rafters have a strong social tendency and throw the most massive parties. There were suddenly good vibrations coming at me from every angle. The whole thing spilled out onto the road and through the forest. You could hear their shrieks. There was good music and plentiful libation, and people of every interesting walk of life you could think of. Lesbians danced wildly, arm in arm, around a great gay bonfire, like children who hadn't had any good reason to celebrate since Christ left Chicago. Every so often I'd ask about Annie.

It seemed she told them all I was crazy, feeling ill, and not up for any formalities. No one knew where she was, but the longer I searched the less I cared to find her.

Lee Donegan was the first familiar face I saw. He had a band of large-chested Romanian palm readers practicing fortune-telling on him, and I tried to intervene and say someone should call the cops before the limo driver went rampaging. I thought gypsies were nothing more than transient thieves— some are. One tried to bite me when I pulled Lee aside. I was still a bit loose-legged and in too delicate a condition to adequately defend myself against the leathery skag's advances.

"What happened to *you*?" he asked.

"I don't exactly know," I told him.

"Are you sick?"

"I'm not sick."

But I surely wasn't well, and the gypsies were quick to speculate.

Lee was having a field day with them. He was always in the mood for a dalliance, and must have thought he hit the jackpot when one, in particular, allowed him to penetrate their ranks. This gypsy was not a skag at all. He kissed her.

She said it was clear that I was on an important quest. "What's her name?" the pretty gypsy asked. I described Annie down to the last detail while Lee went back to toying with her. She never took her eyes off of me.

If I were anything like Lee, and not such a loyal devotee, I'd have responded to that longing look with clear capitulation. It was a stare recognized universally between women and men. She was lovely in a cosmic sense.

The gypsies kindly shared their drinks and recommended marijuana, psychedelic mushrooms, and other broad-spectrum treatments I'd never even heard of to cure my distress. Soon we were all barking mad. I was somewhat indifferent when the skag said that the name Annie meant grace, or divine human assistance.

That was very significant, the pretty gypsy added.

"Are you reading the future?" I asked her.

She said, "I could, but it will cost you."

I gave her what was left in my pocket: a handful of bottle caps and my last twenty. I'd already given Dave the rest for parts. Then she asked for the truth. It was a more hefty deposit.

I told her in one long breath that I'd ended up in Maine because I wanted to be a writer instead of a used car salesman; I followed Annie to cure writer's block, and because she wasn't obsessed with commissions and having children the way Kelsey was. The prospect of a lesbian wedding seemed stimulating enough, but Annie was a liar. We were trapped. Her friends castigated me; none of them were veritable souls, and the whole world seemed more hopeless than the day I'd gotten divorced and went on the internet in search of someone new.

Lee chuckled while his companion stared. Then the sooth-sayer spoke.

"Be careful what you wish for," she proffered, snickering too, and the Romanians quickly moved on, having swindled us both out of cash and all our good sense.

I knew Lee heard too much, and in light of everything, perhaps he thought he had a better chance with Annie. It should've concerned me, but it didn't. We now had the future in hand, as cryptic and chintzy as it ever was. The night was alive and so were we.

As we went in search of more enlightenment, there was a great inevitable commotion inside, and the front door of the cabin swung open. I saw the limo driver emerge holding Dave by the scruff of his thin neck, having resorted to the pure shock-and-awe tactics he spoke of. "Wouldn't you be sorry," Dave shouted as Guy flung him over the railing into the front yard shrubs like a contentious delinquent flogged into submission.

Dave responded by throwing a large stone, and then emerged covered in leafy debris and wielding an empty Moxie bottle, which he threatened to smash over the limo driver's thick Italian skull.

All manner of strange populace had come hither to witness this encounter: bear-faced lunatics, clairvoyants, freaks with curious scars, and Annie. They all craned their necks and then stepped aside as Sweat Lodge Ted pushed through, wearing a full Zuni headdress. The music stopped. He claimed his rightful place among the crowd to keep the peace. The limo driver temporarily suspended his tear, perhaps out of sheer curiosity, while the Grand Poobah dispensed New Age wisdom on the utopian brotherhood of mankind, telling stories that he obviously made up as he went along.

Ted said the universe was all interconnected—synaptic, strange, and surreal.

"We are tadpoles of the cosmos," he proclaimed, "and there are no coincidences. We are all a product of circumstance and evolution, and are precisely where we were meant to be at this, or any, moment. Therefore, we must be at peace and let spirits guide our hearts and minds. We mustn't be afraid or threaten violence against one another, or covet earthly possessions or even fancy limousines."

Tabitha emerged with the broken djembe and began to pound with a slow steady rhythm reminiscent of some long-lost language that spoke of brainsickness and unity. Ted made his rounds with a cactus pipe. The sound was bottomless and hollow. It seemed to emanate from deep within our collective conscious, and before long, we were all back in fair spirits. Even Guy, who spent the night communicating with a higher power through significant chemical interference, was suddenly pacific. He sat completely motionless, staring not at us, but through us, as we fraternized around him.

His beloved car had been returned at that same time, not noticeably worse for the wear. "Just take it," he said absently, and within seconds Lee was tethered to the wheel calling for us to join him.

The pretty gypsy called shotgun as the three of us sprinted toward the limo. Annie led the mad dash and snatched the front seat first. When she did, the gypsy didn't protest. Neither did I. Somehow jealousy didn't enter into the equation; I was too preoccupied.

When we reached the limousine, she said her name was Aishé. What a perfectly uncommon name! I repeated it back, *ay-she*, so I wouldn't forget. How could I? She had long shiny hair that matched her big dark eyes and strange nomadic energy. It called to me. Possessed by some terrifying force, and peyote, I jumped into the back with her and then hung on for dear life. We rolled like two jubilant, unfettered pearls in an oyster shell as the huge cruiser took off, charging through the turns toward whatever destination Lee had in mind.

It was so dark we couldn't see. Aishé opened the moon roof so we could both squeeze ourselves through and glimpse the forest whirring by and all the scattered stars overhead, which were just as far out and impervious as we were.

I said, "This should be our mantra: live free or die!"

It felt like freedom.

That precise moment seemed to make up for the rest of them, without any explanation at all. We screamed choruses at the top of our lungs and banged on the hard vinyl landau roof like Tabitha and her old folk drum. Lee and Annie were up front doing God knows what. He was wily as hell, probably using my own words against me in an effort to drive a wedge between us and get laid. I wasn't especially troubled. When Aishé and I ran out of breath, the two of them joined in and took up the chant where we left off.

"Faster . . . faster," panted Aishé.

The engine roared, straining to keep up with the extreme demands of four cranked-up loons, and we shot out broadside onto a paved mountain road amidst a cloud of dust. Two of Guy's wire rims went sailing off over a steep embankment, and I knew in the morning there'd be hell to pay for losing those. Lee struggled to maintain any kind of even keel as we quickly leaned hard to the right, and then left to compensate and keep the thing on four wheels.

"All ahead!" Lee shouted, and the engine roared once more, beginning to knock as we gathered speed, daring consequence to intervene on a night when Aishé foretold no harm would befall us.

She tilted back to get a better look at me in the light of the moon as her hair blew wild and free. Then she pulled me close. I angled in and Aishé spoke authentically and directly, penetrating my restless soul. "Trust you are on your way," she said.

Lee and Annie didn't hear it.

"On my way to what?" I asked.

"*Soarta*," she replied.

It was clearly something cosmic, but the obnoxious carousing of our endeared had drowned out the question when I asked her what exactly *soarta* meant.

Annie said she knew just where Lee was taking us—for some raft guide initiation on high that required bravery, skill, and luck. Before long we'd leveled off, having neared the spot at the top of a mountain. We were staring hundreds, if not thousands, of feet down, beyond a narrow roadside guardrail into the abyss.

The world outside our window seemed to melt into the long black chasm. Soon the brakes squealed sharply as Lee brought the wasted limousine to a sudden stop. One minute more and I'd have probably capsized if I discovered what, in my hallucination, the universe and Aishé were trying to say. But we'd found that wild intangible precipice Lee'd been searching for.

My heart pounded with anticipation as we all got out to fill the great silent territory with the sounds of our debauchery. Pharmacon and freedom is a powerful and highly addictive combination. My mind was still racing through deserted hairpins, taking me far from Maine and then back again in waves that threatened to wreck me.

To demonstrate our lust for love, life, and recklessness, we'd have to balance upon the guardrail, walking a knife's edge between this world and the next for at least fifty feet.

This feat required focus.

Lee was the first to go. Without hesitation, he ran the length of rusty metal, three inches wide, with both hands in pockets and a Marlboro steaming between his lips. He didn't care about anything. We all cheered him on. If he slipped or stumbled it'd be certain death, but that was the point of the exercise so far as I could tell: to weed out those unworthy of fortuity and spiritual command. Then, when he made it to the end without falling off into limbo, we exploded!

"That's it!" Annie exclaimed, and the gypsy girl ran barefoot on solid ground, with her big boobs bouncing the whole way over, to congratulate him.

She refused to take the rail herself no matter what the chakras had divined.

Lee tried putting his arms around her and called her chicken for taking the safe route. "Are you a sorceress or not?" he asked, and Aishé cracked him twice, close-fisted, in the mouth for calling her a phony.

"No fair!" Lee protested. He lost his cigarette and more in the quarrel.

Aishé pushed him back and then let him have it, unleashing the evil eye in a string of uninterruptable Romanian imprecations. "What does that mean?" Lee asked.

Aishé told him it meant a lot of things. For one, his power over women would abruptly cease at sunup, which was too long of a turnaround, as it ended up. He was going to have to make the most of his ability while it lasted. To break her witchery, he'd need to apologize for his affront and find a gypsy grave to pray over and then cast his own spell. I'd read somewhere that although rare, gypsy curses are sudden and very powerful.

Lee shrugged it off. He was unimpressed. He only wanted more liquor—and to leave an indelible mark upon this world and on everyone and everything he contacted. We all wanted that.

The rail was hard to see in the dark. Annie nervously stepped up; she was next to go. It didn't help that Lee and his gypsy were quickly back in synch, perched at the other end, making catcalls and groping each other in the moonlight.

Lee hollered, "We don't have all night!"

"Be quiet," shouted Annie as she took her first step out of spite and then continued going, putting one foot slowly in front of the other.

She'd obviously pulled it off at some point before. That's the only way they'll let you run the Class 5 on the Penobscot, and she'd mentioned it many times. That flume was roaring somewhere far below in the distance. When she finished, the river gods and I exhaled a billowing, dope-smoky sigh of relief. No one held their breath for me, though. They all lit up like it was New Year's Day and the clock just struck midnight.

I told myself it wasn't hard, just a stupid thing kids do— and you hear about them dying for it all the time. I wasn't afraid of falling. What did I have to lose? So I took the first step, beer in hand. I trusted Aishé, who was watching, not telling me to stop or that I was about to go splat on the rocks down below. It was transcendental, and my soles were like glue that night. In my mind I saw nothing but the rail as I took the next step. The wind blew. It tried blowing me over, but I was centered in deep meditative silence. It was rapture. I stepped again. Then, in spite of consequence and all other consideration, I began to leap as if there was no force in all the universe that could check me. There were profound contemplative narratives flowing through my brain as I then proclaimed, halfway, that I was a glittering god, predestined to change the world with my scribbling.

"They will ponder this for years!" I announced, receiving every word like it was communion in the state of mind that I was in. But the channel was cut off at the terminus of the rail, before I could begin to archive everything that I'd discerned.

I hugged Lee and his gypsy anyway, to celebrate, and having discharged my writer's block, I sent my contract and any future at Stager over the rail into oblivion. Annie was spectating close by. She came running to testify to the accomplishment, claiming we were inseparably connected, adding my name to the list of those who'd gone before me. Raft guides. She proceeded to name them.

"I love you, sweetie," she said, because now she thought we were kindred—guides in one form or another—through to the bitter end. Wherever that quay was, I told Annie that it was drawing closer.

It wasn't long before they were all asleep in the back of the limo as the current drew us onward in the direction of a mammoth churn. Destiny. It propelled us forward toward a future destination that had always seemed elusive. Now it was about to come crashing into view. I sensed it.

And for the first time in my life I began to understand that the master plan required much more than hard work, alcohol, and ambition to get over the hump. Few aspiring writers ever get past it. Those that do know the risk and sacrifice involved. But there was no use trying to rationalize or speculate on a night like that.

There wasn't a cloud in the sky, so I just soaked it all in and let it sweep me along.

It was a hell of a view.

Chapter 7

IN THE EARLY MORNING, ANNIE CONFESSED everything in one of those crazy dreams before dawn while Lee and his gypsy slept close beside her, huddled on the cold, cracked leather. I wasn't sleeping. Instead, I listened while Lee joined in on the unconscious avowal. He caressed Annie's arm and snored like a grizzly. Then I began scheming once again.

There was reason to believe that I'd been poisoned the day before, just like the limo driver. In my clearer head, I narrowed the list of suspects, then came to the conclusion that it was Lee Donegan, not Dave, who'd dosed me. He did it to keep me out of contention so he could have his way with Annie. She called out his name.

Perhaps she'd rebuked his advances at first. Maybe she didn't. In all her mumbling, it was hard to discern a timeline. But the facts remained. If we stayed in Maine much longer, curse or no curse, we might never get out. Had it not been for the gypsy, I might not have lived to tell about it.

Annie had begun to describe the sexual part of their encounter when I sprang out of the front seat for air. I took Lee's Marlboros with me and, in case I puked, grabbed a beer to wash out the taste.

It was Aishé who followed me outside into the darkness to smoke, sensing some immutable vibration. She climbed through the open moon roof, careful not to disturb the babbling lovebirds. We puffed, following a trail of scattered cans in the dark back to the rusty rail, and watched the sunrise over the Penobscot without saying a word for the longest time.

Then she whispered, "Give me your hand."

I threw my cigarette over. We watched it fall all the way down to the crushing whitewater a mile below. I offered up a sweaty, trembling palm.

Her hands were soft, calm, and steady as they grasped mine. She studied the lines and saw what the future held in store. Then she closed her dark brown, beautiful gypsy eyes. I asked her what the universe had divined.

Aishé shook with the revelation.

"You've got a longer way to go," she said.

"Toward what?" I questioned.

"*Soarta.*"

She said it meant fate. Mine was especially significant. She told me there'd be danger and heartache up ahead.

"How do I avoid it?"

"You can't."

"Then what's the point?"

"Of what?"

"Of prophecy," I said, demanding answers.

She said, "You wouldn't understand if I told you."

That was the truth.

Looking back, I wouldn't have understood a lot of things she could've said. And if she had explained it all—the future— well, then I might have tried changing everything, which would've been utterly futile. There's no changing course once destiny's been evoked, she explained, like a waterfall that draws you over. I'd paddled toward it instead of away from it for the past three months, stirring river gods and others. Now it threat- ened to smash me at the bottom.

I was terrified. The sound of rushing water has always made me nervous. I'd have turned back around if I could, right then, toward Stager, safer shores, and the rest. Aishé knew it. She tried steering me back on course.

In an effort to distract me, she kissed me abruptly on the cheek. It was a gentle kiss. I'd have planted mine further left, on the lips, if she'd allowed, but that would've led to other tempta- tions that Aishé didn't foresee.

Together we watched the new day reveal itself. Soon the last star disappeared. "Where will you go when you leave?" I asked.

"Anywhere but here," she said, staring off toward the endless horizon.

"That'd be fine."

"Should I take you with me?" Aishé said, smiling. She laughed. "Tell me, where would you like to go now, huh? See the whole world, huh?"

I nodded and pictured it just as it was, cold and empty for miles in every direction. But there was so much more that I couldn't see, and suddenly there was not much left to keep me from going and experiencing everything, the way all the great writers did. "What about Las Vegas?" I proposed.

"Yes, of course," Aishé said. "But you wouldn't like it very much."

She told me she worked there as a dancer once—not a call girl, but a dancer. "I know what you're thinking," she said nudging my shoulder. "Most people are judgmental, but if I turned tricks, I'd call it that."

"I'm not judging you."

"Nah. I can see that."

"What else do you see?"

I wanted her to tell me everything, even if I couldn't understand. Did I really leave Stager? Did I end up alone? An alcoholic? Suicide? Did I not write the novel? That would've been worse. Was that the heartache?

"I can see that you don't know the first thing about the world," she replied.

She showed me what was left of the name tattooed on her right arm. "I know about the things that boy in the limousine did, but that's the world you think you're missing. Las Vegas, huh? It's never what you hope for."

But I hoped for it anyways.

Lee had told Aishé all about the past with Annie. He'd admitted to some things not even listed in her journal. Rufilin was apparently part of his modus operandi.

Beyond that, she told me she was on her way back from the Midwest with the fading scars to prove she couldn't be broken, bound, or branded by anything or anyone at all. Lee was just an amusement, no different from any of the other men she'd known. She was wiser now, but said that didn't make it any better.

She showed me the earthen grit beneath her nails, and said the road was her home. She'd tried settling down, but it only made her feel lashed and lonely.

"Then we're one and the same," I said.

"Nah. Not hardly," Aishé replied. "You're different."

I tried convincing her otherwise, to prove that I was worthy and just as desperate for insight and latitude as she was. Not just drifting, but *soarta*. Aishé shook her head.

She said, "You've already got it in the palm of your hand."

Then she released me from her grip. I studied each of my fingers and the intricate patchwork of ridges and exes that stretched down to the wrist, wondering what it all meant.

Aishé laughed. She mentioned that Lee left the keys to the limousine dangling from its ignition switch. "Freedom is a state of mind," she said. "That's *your* story—I'm telling you the future."

I pondered the revelation, considering the breadth of my present state of entrapment and others. I thought of all my friends in Hazard, the car dealership, Annie, and the familiar feeling that I'd come to associate with being perpetually caged. Now I weighed my chances for a clean break.

Aishé waited for me to decide. I wanted her to tell me more. I wanted to be the bright pink feather that she twirled between her fingers, tied up in her long brown hair. I pictured the open road and making wild gypsy love with her in the middle of some deserted highway beneath the stars, just as I knew it could have been—how it would have been had she not had it right from the very beginning. She smiled reassuringly, and then I understood at least some of what she was trying to say.

Lee emerged to take a leak, and I signaled to Aishé that I was ready. It was time to make our move. Right away she threatened to pounce. To this day, whenever I catch the scent of stale cigarettes in the early morning, I think of her that way: poised, pretty, and reckless because I needed her to be. I told her I had a plan for the maneuver, praying God and the universe would forgive me for what I was about to do.

God is not hard to find in the wild. Whatever you conceive him to be, He is transformative and near for those who petition Him—the twinkle in deep dark eyes. I hoped He had a sense of humor.

Aishé knew the odds were stacked against us. Lee Donegan was a formidable adversary, though I assumed she, having prophesized the outcome, decided to side with the winning team. She grabbed a nearby stone.

"I'll bash him over the head quick," she whispered, but I had other ideas. One way or the other our unspoken plan was clear: ditch the mangy raft guide, pray for salvation, and then bolt!

I scuttled quickly over to the limousine to take up a strategic position, concealed by its massive boot end, and motioned for Aishé to join me. Then, when the moment was right, we jumped in, laughing like children, and locked all the doors. Annie was still passed out cold in the back seat.

It took me several tries with the enormous stretcher to make a complete about-face. At one point, I was certain that we were all going over when the left front tire skipped over the edge of the embankment. Annie was still in a daze and had no concept of the peril we were in.

"Hold still," I told Aishé as I threw the transmission into reverse.

The tire spun in the loose gravel. I felt the limo tip forward, then abruptly shoot back, as the tire gained traction and we smashed into the mountain. I slammed it into drive as rocks rained down from above, then I steered hard to starboard and made the final turn with inches to spare.

"Where's Lee?" Annie asked.

I saw him running toward us. He was getting closer. Then I floored it.

Aishé and I were both too caught up to notice the expression on his face as we sped past. We were bursting with rapture, like modern-day pirates on the high side of a great ocean tide. I saw him trailing in the rearview, lost in a cloud of dust. I turned a corner, and we were gone. I had sailed away with Lee's pearl.

There's nothing like racing down backcountry roads in a stolen limousine with a good gypsy by your side. It was at once cathartic—more potent than a drug—and the closest to redemption that I have ever been.

We headed south toward home and passed the cabin in a blur. Annie was still questioning the sudden turn of events as Aishé tuned up the radio, and soon the great North Woods were nothing but a strange, fuzzy memory more distant with every mile.

I had Aishé crawl through to the back to search for provisions before we got on the interstate. Then, with some assurances that she'd procured a few warm beers, I put the pedal down and we commenced with the extraction, channeling a slow, steady twang on an AM band for the next three hundred miles.

A highway cop followed us from Portland to Portsmouth. He was right on our tail. Annie was convinced he was on to us.

"Stupid musker," Aishé said. "Hold steady!"

I gripped the wheel and passed my beer to Annie.

Aishé told me not to worry. "If he tries anything, I'll jump and run. Then you take off in the opposite direction with your girl!"

"What if he catches you?"

"But he won't," said Aishé.

"What if he doesn't take the bait? What if he shoots?"

"Then you better be ready to fight!" she said, grinning.

At this point I'd gotten the massive Lincoln all over the road from nerves, practically straddling the dashed line, and

I was, without question, in a sufficient state of inebriation to warrant further investigation.

Two miles to the border. It wasn't a race; it was a damned, desperate charge for deliverance. We were running on empty. The old engine spit and sputtered. It was empty too.

Aishé shouted "*Soartă*" when we reached mile marker one, and we counted down from there together.

"Zero point nine, zero point eight . . . "

We passed the sign welcoming visitors to Maine—*The Way Life Should Be*—and there before us was the state of New Hampshire, which never seemed so Arcadian.

The trooper sped up.

I yelled, "Live free or die!" as the border came into view.

He was driving right beside us at this point, peering at us in the side view mirror.

"Do you know what they do to people like me in prison?" I screamed.

"Be calm," Aishé said.

We were almost there, having witnessed the elucidation of dreams at the uttermost bizarre edges of life as I knew it then. I couldn't wait to tell my story.

I decided on some changes for the future, which was more like an impromptu negotiation with the universe in exchange for getting us over those last five hundred feet of unholy ground. It was imperative that the people in charge realized the same possibility that I then saw laid out before me, the one Aishé foretold and I interpreted. It flashed before my eyes.

I promised *it—soarta*, God, the universe, or whatever force—that I'd follow the signs when I got home. I'd make amends if I had to, for the sake of liberty, if He, She, They, or Them let us through, blinding the trooper and sustaining our fuel supply until we were safely across state lines.

Lord, don't fail me now!

Having said that, in those last few seconds on the run, my thoughts turned toward other hopeful investments. The pretty gypsy there beside me was unafraid and beholden to no one. She kept her right hand on the door handle the whole time, ready to thrust herself out into the fray. Consequence and whatever ramifications our chronicles brought about were no matter to her. There was no sign of repentance or subjugation in her.

Annie shouted for me to pull over. She was terrified and saw the officer on the radio, probably calling for backup.

I stayed steady on the throttle, kept all my options open—ecclesial and otherwise—and waited for the trooper to make his move.

The New Hampshire state line was just ahead.

We were upon it in seconds as Heaven or some other strange fortuity opened up its gates to reveal what was written, and all I had yet to write about. The cop heeded the call.

I saw him turn off at the last median crossover.

"Hallelujah!" I exclaimed, as Aishé was searching for a lighter to spark a celebratory joint. "What are you, fucking crazy?"

"I believe you both are!" Annie said.

She was right—not only because I handed Aishé a pack of matches with the trooper still visible in the rearview, but also for my mad, ecstatic belief that I had anything to offer Zion that it didn't already have.

We took the next exit to fill up in Manchester. There was some sort of festival going on, and suddenly we were surrounded on all sides by throngs of dedicated weekenders and yuppies haymaking in what was left of the midday sun. These people had no concept of *soarta*. They believed in Congress, capital, and the Pope.

I told Aishé I knew all about these kinds of people. I dealt with them every day, every time a big black Suburban or Volvo or Buick drove onto the lot. They were all pretentious snobs—clones of one another—with the same spurious dink ambitions, or with clutches of loud ugly children to help justify their existence in this sad world. I swore God only cloned dumb assholes, for some reason. And the assholes didn't seem to mind. Aishé shook her head in disgust, rolled the window down, and let her fingers swim in the cool breeze.

"These are not your kind," she said.

No, they weren't. And I pitied them more than ever because, even if I was technically a fugitive now, two steps from the gallows, at least I had the sense enough to try and avoid the noose. Their heads were already in it.

I looked at Aishé, who, for the first time since I'd known her, seemed melancholic and distant. "Have the oracles suddenly gone silent?" I asked.

Her sad expression told me everything.

Outside, the dink revival continued. Every arriviste in all of New England came out to take pictures of themselves drinking pumpkin-flavored ales for the internet. No one rational drinks gourd-flavored beer.

"Just listen to them!" I said.

They sounded like Paul Stager's swinish patrons, dazzling over foot-longs, fighting to stand in long lines so they could fill their enormous bellies. It was the saddest, and most hysterical, thing I've ever seen. What a circus!

Aishé finally cracked a smile. The world, to her, was just one big spinning tilt-a-whirl, and we were spinning. Smoke poured from the cabin. We drifted on fumes. I could see that she was building up to something as we pulled into the service station, dizzy from the weed and from watching the insane spectacle pass by at an unsafe speed, like all of life was just a carnival ride. She could get off any time she wanted.

Annie, on the other hand, was utterly oblivious and couldn't sense the undertow. She asked if we were stopping for lunch.

"Yes, of course," I said, and asked her to bring me however many hot dogs they had inside. I was starving. Annie was hungry too. She sweetly obliged.

Aishé gathered her things. It was time for her to keep moving on. Her only hunger was the highway, and it called to her like an insatiable growl, the way my stomach groaned for cured meat. I knew somehow it wasn't the last time I'd see her, but the feeling was no less doleful.

"Tell me something," she said, with the same sad look on her face as when we first pulled off the interstate. We both got out. "Will you ever confront her?"

"Who?"

"Your girl," Aishé responded waggishly.

"Annie wouldn't begin to understand fate, truth, or anything," I said as the gypsy collected her things. "Where are you going?" I asked.

We met at the front of the car, which was thoroughly flogged and still ticking from the heat. She pushed me firmly with both hands on my chest until I fell back against the hood. Then she kissed me again, this time hard on the lips, for encouragement. She said she didn't want me to freak out.

"About what?" I asked.

"You have a delicate nature," she said, getting around to her point.

It was just that she wasn't, in the strictest sense, a *bona fide* sage.

"It's not something you're born with," Aishé explained. Prophesying was a cultivated, complicated craft, like learning how to swindle.

"You witch!" I exclaimed. "Are you even Romanian?"

"How are you such a fool?" Aishé snickered. She didn't wait for me to answer. "You're a damn miracle, I swear! The way you had that highway musker going. That cop would've torn us to shreds!"

"I thought we were in the hands of destiny—*soarta*!"

"We were," she insisted. "How do you think we got here?"

"Bullshit!" I exclaimed just as Annie emerged from the gas station with her arms full. She wanted nothing to do with the debate, laid the hot dogs on my lap, and steered clear.

"You're going to end up a fat tourist," Aishé said laughing.

What did I care? They seemed happy enough chasing their tails.

"But you can't!"

"Why not?"

"Because every word I've told to you was the truth."

She wanted me to believe her, and somehow I did.

"You could've gotten me killed!"

But that wasn't what Aishé had foreseen. She said I was her first legitimate prognostication. That's partly what made me so different. It was hard for her to explain. She'd tried interpreting the signs. They came through in waves and then left her wanting more, to find out how the story ended, when the visions faded.

"How *does* it end?" I asked her.

Aishé said she wasn't sure. She only knew that I'd write it.

I promised to try.

"You have to!" Aishé insisted. "You will."

She stared deeply. Her gaze was wilder, and more fierce, than any of what she'd commanded or prophesied about—an impression I knew, even then, I could never recapture or outrun. Then she turned and was off in a steady stream of pastels and plaid.

If I'd known she was gone for good I'd have asked for her number, at least. I wasted a half hour there, eating hot dogs with Annie and thinking Aishé might come back. But it was just my imagination running wild. It wasn't fate.

Annie eventually asked what we were waiting for, a tow truck?

I told her not to worry. Guy's limousine was still drivable, so far as I could tell.

"Are you feeling okay?" I asked.

Annie said yes, but the journey had taken a toll on both of us.

I climbed into the driver's seat. She joined me, now in the front. She slid herself across the bench and threw an arm over my shoulder so that we could ride hip to hip.

"Where are we? I mean, you and I?" she asked.

I wasn't certain of that. I wasn't exactly certain of anything. But we had a tank full of gas, cigarettes on the dash, and—for the moment, all things considered—it was almost better than certitude. Almost.

I said, "I think we are on the brink of total annihilation." And that was not at all dramatized.

"I think you just need to relax," Annie replied.

"Is that what you told Lee?" I questioned. She seemed as clueless as ever. "When he dosed me with Rufilin?"

"What in the world are you talking about?" she coughed.

"Don't deny it!" I shouted without revealing everything that I knew to be self-evident—all that I'd read, or how I'd come to know it.

"You're insane!" Annie countered deftly.

That might've been the truest thing she'd ever said.

I turned the tired old engine over. It started. That in itself was a phenomenon. I didn't waste any more time in wonder. I took it as a sign and pointed us south, once again toward home—Exit 285 on the interstate and the dawning of our next big disaster.

Chapter 8

THE LONELY HIGHWAY OUTSIDE MANCHESTER shot straight ahead in two long, dilapidated parallel lines that stretched all the way to Boston. I continued south, driving toward that giant monstrosity I knew was out there. When the highway signs assured me that it'd passed, I leaned right, with both hands held steady on the wheel, and followed the shortest route out of that Godforsaken territory.

Annie was back asleep. She was a hard one to impress. At the time, I attributed her general malaise to the fact that I was a lowly used car salesman, not a rafter or a cowboy. I tried vigorously in those days to stimulate her interest in me by telling stories about how different life would be for us after the novel came out. I was telling one of those, instead of bitching about the weekend in Maine, when she started dozing off. Not even the highway troopers we'd passed, who pointed radar detectors from the median, could get her blood flowing.

I missed the gypsy already. Aishé had it all put together—or faked it at least. At least she *tried* to fake it. Annie didn't seem to try very hard, except where subterfuge and saving her own skin was concerned. And now that she was safe, she left navigating the rest of the way through the aftermath up to me.

It was in that silent flak where I felt my chest begin to heave. It was an unrelenting constriction that had everything to do with Annie and her camouflaged affections for Lee. My attention swerved from avoiding enormous potholes, for the sake of Guy's three remaining wire rims, and leaned toward deliberation. It was a panicked thought process that began with my doubts about any legal precedence for seeking annulment under those circumstances and ended with me being utterly alone if such a thing was possible.

Here's the dilemma: I've been called a serial monogamist, among other things. The fact is, I could see no way to thrive as a single man. What good use was all of my effort and commotion if there wasn't a beneficiary there to notice, or object, or offer comfort in the way of sex? Un-attachment is just another word for masturbation. It's utterly futile, especially for a writer. So I thought about the options, just as I'd always done.

Kelsey was a backup plan, albeit the last one that came to mind. As it turned out, Annie was right about that fact all along, though had it not been for such discord in the North Woods I might have overlooked it. I tried calling her then to test out the waters.

You can learn awful lot about regret from one weekend in Maine. I was wholly disenchanted, and at least partly wasted, but more resolute than I had been in the months since Kelsey and I split up over matters slightly less disturbing than those currently wracking my brain. Not the least of those included the distinct possibility that I'd gotten remarried much too soon to a polyamorous bonbon too sweet to tell the lips of one man from another. Annie now most likely dreamed of him while I carted her out of harm's way. That's how I rationalized it.

As the phone rang, I started having flashbacks and visions, and visions of flashbacks of wretched gurneys and disorderly hospital herds, and that gone look on Kelsey's face when I said that I was leaving.

◆ ◆ ◆

She knew I meant it this time.

They said it was my fault in some roundabout way, first for keeping her up so late the previous night, which exacerbated her nervous condition. She cheated with the raft guide who I first encountered in the waiting room. He was no orderly. He was the one who brought her in and was there now, along with her sister, at the hospital bedside, to help explain it.

Kelsey said the long hours at Stager, and my hopeless abandon for the sake of writing to change our stars, drove her to it. The affair happened, of course, while I was at the damn dealership. She said she was feeling much better—relieved, actually—and that it was for the best, the way everything came to be revealed. Like Aaron, she wouldn't have had the heart to tell me otherwise, had it not happened the way that it did.

"How long has this been going on?" I asked.

"You've got a lot to live for," Kelsey stated.

The Mountain Chief nodded along. He started to explain that she'd had a very traumatic episode.

"In the act?" I injected.

"She fell off the bed and knocked her head," he responded.

And that was the whole story. They waited for *me* to atone.

He said, "I'm going to take good care of her."

"Hey fuck you, man," I replied. But before I had the chance to strangle him with the twisted mess of intravenous tubeage, Kelsey's sister stepped in.

She was a highly perceptive three-time divorcée who played both sides like the Devil, a succubus with very little left in the way of charm.

She said I should have been more supportive, more sensitive, and less of a prick when it all came to light. Her sister called me a prick when I spat in her face. Maybe she was right.

Then I freaked, and started naming all the hypothetical children. Don't tell me she hadn't informed the raft guide about those. I could see by the puzzled look on his face that she hadn't. What did he know about support and sensitivity? Kelsey pondered this revelation also, and I think for a brief second contemplated trying to suck me back in. Not this time.

♦ ♦ ♦

All the nostalgia brought me temporarily back to my senses as Annie began to nuzzle me with her head laid on my shoulder.

I didn't wait for the ringing to stop. Kelsey hadn't answered. I didn't leave a message. I didn't know what else to say besides, "It's me, and I don't give a damn what anyone thinks about it," which was exactly the kind of thing her sister was talking about. And I might have still loved Kelsey, in some irrational way; but then again, I was too drunk and defiled to be certain.

Then I saw the radio tower out of the dusty driver-side window, up ahead on the right-hand side of the road where I once pulled off for no reason other than peacockery on our way home from visiting some of Kelsey's friends in Connecticut. She'd told them all about me. They were skeptical and unwelcoming too. We'd argued the entire time up and back, as usual. I'd pointed toward the tall steel structure and told Kelsey I was once again suicidal. It was daring me to climb!

I recalled that she'd bundled up for the ordeal. It was freezing that night. I remembered her trying to stop me from getting out, going to the very top, where I'd sworn to disavow this world and then leap. She shouted various admonishments. That didn't deter me. Then when I finally got up there and my ears, nose, and heart were all completely numb, she was shivering right beside. It was an impressive gesture, which kept me stable. We sat down on the catwalk with our backs against a rail, resonating with the great magnetic hum of electric waves pulsing through our bodies, permeating the atmosphere and circling the earth ten times per second. It was palpable, and even she was silent and reverent. But it didn't last.

It was clear if Annie and I were going to make it the rest of the way, if for no other reason than some form of conquest, then I'd have to steer straight, keep my mind on the road ahead, and focus. It was easier said than done, but a half mile later, the tower was out of sight—and so went the memory that'd come with it. There was nothing else to see for miles.

The next few hours were a sad, solitary blur. Annie was still sleeping. I didn't realize until then how empty the road could be when it's just you and a thousand foreign cars jostling for position, with nothing good on the radio and no one cognizant or caring enough to change the channel.

Annie never liked my taste in music. She was always a witless country kind of girl who believed "Proud Mary" was a song about people getting bombed on a float trip. I swore it wasn't, but she professed veracity like a pontiff, and possessed a great propensity for seeing things her way and staying committed even when it didn't make sense. I told myself she deserved someone who could do the same. Not Lee Donegan. A cowboy, perhaps?

I might have learned how to better rope the wind if the truth about her wasn't always stranger and more perilous than any fiction I could've imagined. As a writer, that would make it both harder to leave her and harder to stay. I knew, because I studied both scenarios carefully as the miles passed by in a blur and hadn't come to any sober unwavering conclusions when we crossed into the state of New York.

Now it was all I could do to keep on driving, as what started out as profligacy turned steadily back toward predicament and I ran out of cigarettes. Then, somewhere near Poughkeepsie, a couple hours from Hazard, reality set in. My heart pounded over what to do with a wasted, stolen limousine after we got there.

I instantly called on Wade Balshi, the only dissident I knew who might well have been fully decamped or living off the grid ever since the whole Stager ordeal had him jammed up with the state police. They let him off easy, though, considering the charges, and I wondered what remedy he'd have for fixing the mess I'd gotten myself into.

The last I knew he was holed up, nesting like a fugitive in his so-called retirement.

He lived in the hills outside of town, on a property I found quite easily once I was in the vicinity. I'd been to his shanty once before—to collect his forfeited dealership regalia, following the arraignment.

Life had him fucked up. That was obvious from the moment I first turned down the driveway marked with a dozen or more homemade yard signs painted red, warning of all kinds of mortal harm. I knew for certain that I had the right place when I read one that said "ALL SALESMEN WILL BE SHOT ON SIGHT!" I had to go past several of these to reach the Captain's rusted trailer, which was parked right in the middle of a muddy lane, presumably in the precise location where the truck that'd been pulling it had broken down.

When we pulled up Wade emerged almost immediately, carrying a cleaver and wearing an old Stager Auto World button-down he hadn't surrendered. It had blood stains on the sleeves. He was attempting to decapitate an insubordinate chicken, which he called by name. Travis had lost half of his feathers in the ordeal.

"Look at you," he said to the bird. "You're ungrateful!"

The chicken paused and cocked its head to the side.

"Grab him!" Wade exclaimed as I, not more than three steps from the cockpit, instinctively lunged toward the unsuspecting fowl. It let out a horrific screech as it was caught, and the Captain lopped off its head.

"You never stop by," he said then, as if he'd just greeted me at the door with a firm handshake and we weren't suddenly forehead to forehead, after all those years, with a pool of blood and quivering feathers between us.

"Good to see you, my boy," he said.

"I'm having some trouble," I told him.

"Yes, I can see that," the Captain replied.

He jumped right up to assess damages, walking around the limousine as any well-trained appraiser would. He kicked the tires, peered inside, and forgot all about his supper, which hadn't yet stopped squirming in my trembling hands.

Annie had finally come to at this point, but pretended to remain asleep for reasons I understood without her having to explain.

"Let's go inside," Wade said.

I followed him in; I thought to straighten up and to strategize, but the rules of strange social etiquette intervened when the Captain offered a sample of some very dangerous tonic he'd procured. It was imperative to him that I try the stuff. He drank straight from the bottle and, as not to seem discourteous, I sipped from the chipped glass he gave me, which he pulled from the sink and wiped out with his two crimson-stained, calloused fingers.

The accommodations left a lot to be desired. I imagined my sad, solitary future looking a lot like his, pressed between four polyvinyl walls—the kind of thing you'd see in a porn shop bathroom. And the Captain had a dog, Tom Waits, named after his favorite singer. It was obviously drunk.

"What's wrong with this animal?" I asked.

The Captain said, "Tom likes the taste of vomit."

His was always rife with liquid tonic, which the dog seemed to appreciate. Tom was addicted, in fact, according to Wade.

"We have a lot of catching up to do," he said.

I nodded, and then tried to keep up with the pace of conversation from there. The Captain had a lot to say. His eyes were wide and fierce—hysterical at times—and, depending upon the subject, mad with rage over one revelation or another.

Wade said he was supposed to be dead. The doctors all thought so, but no one could've been more surprised or disappointed than he was when he woke up inside a mortuary body bag. He scratched his way out and kicked open the freezer door, having glimpsed the hereafter. "It was a beautiful sight," he said. "They had a casino!"

The Captain was a dedicated gambler on both sides of eternity. He played blackjack exclusively and had just hit 21 on a double down, sitting at a table with God, when his heart started beating again. After that he found it hard to assimilate.

"How so?" I asked cautiously.

He said, "Well, I wasn't about to go back to into sales, if that's what you're asking."

Evidently, the afterlife had made quite an impression on him. It was strange. I'd never pegged the Captain for a religious man. He said he learned that lying was the greatest, most indomitable sin. He'd been reborn and walked on eggshells ever since, out of fear some inadvertent transgression might land him in the doghouse eternally. Then he might never return to that crystal casino in the sky.

"They should have left well enough alone," he charged, explaining how the doctors' extraneous measures had a delayed effect that led to his revival and the current predicament.

Now he had no internet and no phone, in an effort to sequester himself from the damnation of the outside world. It was a miracle he made the cut the first time. He wasn't about to test the standard twice.

The handmade signs at the front of the drive served as evidence of this. Salesmen were the worst kind of unfortunate liars out of all the unrighteous offenders, according to Wade. He knew too well from his years of bargaining at Stager. He said the Bible made ample provision for the use of force, as a means of dutiful self-defense. That script seemed rational in his mind. His holy line had been dug into the dirt, and he pitied any fool who tried crossing it. They'd been warned.

I suddenly felt my palms begin to sweat.

"Life's not all that it's cracked up to be," I told him.

He took another swig.

"There are a lot of facts to support that," Wade replied. He filled my glass to the brim and twitched his nostrils as he drew close. "When was the last time you took a damn shower?"

I shrugged.

He chuckled like the madman that he was and continued on with the dissertation, saying my feeble-mindedness and rotten funk were getting us nowhere. "You have to consider the grand scheme!"

I tried explaining that eminent property still parked in the driveway was my reason for being there. It could have me placed in shackles. Before I had the chance to clarify, the Captain cut me off. He said, "I'm sorry to tell you this, my boy, but if you came seeking repair, you won't find it here."

Now, abatement he could offer. That deal came in the form of the liquid he poured out and consumed at every pause, whenever his lips stopped flapping long enough to wrap them around the top of the bottle. He waved it around to make his point appear even more dramatic as he began to sway.

I asked if we should take a few minutes for recovery.

"Never!" he sniped. That was exactly the opposite of what we were going to do. "We'd only end up sniveling. Relapse, it's a trap!"

So we drank even more, toasting that the powers that be might never have their chance to say I told you so.

"Live free or die," I declared, raising my glass.

And the Captain said, "My boy, you've been poisoned."

I agreed.

He said society was to blame for my woolgathering; that Paul Stager, most certainly, was the beneficiary of my naïveté. But not his. Not anymore and never again.

"Fear is not freedom," he instructed.

I had that pusillanimous look about me all the time in those days. Especially then, as he analogized it, to the unscrupulous high-pressure tactics employed to complete a sale.

He was wise to the game and lived off the grid to smite them—the cheats at Stager who'd rejected him, and others who'd all have to drag him out of there in a body bag or risk being murdered themselves for their imprudence if they wanted recompense.

Outside, Annie waited in the wings. Perhaps she was getting a little annoyed about the duration of our all-important pit stop. She was not at all sagacious.

Wade hated anything commissary or rational, and declared himself a laureate of perverted truths. But they were truths nonetheless. These circumstances he continued to catalogue in between glugs.

I didn't have to say much, except when he paused for affirmation. Then I acknowledged him and stayed clear of his fists whenever they clenched and swung wildly through the air like those of a crazed prizefighter. Finally, he'd gotten so far off track that he'd forgotten the point of our meeting: the limousine.

He said, "Now it's time for the show!"

At this point I put the glass down and Wade stumbled over to the door. It was getting dark, so he invited us to stay. I told him Annie was petrified, in no shape for revelry, and there were other considerations.

"Don't you realize that the cops will soon be crawling all over this place?" I exclaimed.

"Then turn the lights off," he commanded, as if the measure was obvious.

And I did whatever he told me to do, both out of fear for our lives and because I had no other option.

Wade was a brilliant strategist, from what I remembered. At Stager he was known as the closer, and it wasn't until his heart attack, when they'd prescribed ketamine for his imbalances, that he'd begun acting weirdly—making indomitable threats and constantly wearing the seafarer's hat for which he eventually became known.

Now he was my only hope, and he was searching for a flashlight. Upon finding one, he placed it on the counter in a plastic grocery bag to diffuse the beam. He said the bluish light was imperceptible from the outside, and suddenly the outward world disappeared.

"Can you see okay?" he asked.

"Yes, I can see," I told him.

Then we were finally getting down to business, discussing contingency plans for what to do with the limousine. The Captain made room for us to sit at a TV table, which doubled as a repository for all his dirty dishes. Everything ended up on the floor, including Wade, who stumbled over a waffle iron. He fell forward, knocking off all the glassware and busting his two front teeth loose on the pantry.

At that very moment Annie, bored of sitting the car, came through the front door. Wade, believing it was the law or some unwelcome peddler, grabbed a double-barrel Savage he had taped beneath the sink. Without hesitation, he fired it twice into the dark.

"Jesus Christ!" I exclaimed.

"Get down!" he said as I heard him reload.

Annie survived by the grace of God, and hit the deck as the Captain unleashed another round of lead.

"Cease fire!" I demanded, and then let Wade have it, striking him across the head with a heavyweight service platter I'd plucked from the kitchen floor.

He staggered and dropped the gun, and I quickly moved to retrieve it.

Now, with the still smoldering barrels pointed squarely at him, I explained the whole situation while he surveyed himself for damages. Annie brushed herself off.

I started with what happened in Maine and ended with my thoughts on what to do with the old heap, having described the terrible, angry disposition of Guy Manchetti. I said that I had nothing to lose, and that I wouldn't hesitate to pull the trigger if Wade even flinched.

"What is it you think will blow over?" he asked. "You think the cops or that wetback will just forget this sometime soon?"

I thought they might if he'd help.

"You're going to need a good attorney," he said, and recommended intense therapy second, along with a full-spectrum treatment for my psychosis.

Wizard oil, he insisted, was the only true, long-term remedy for what ailed me. It tasted like turpentine and by then had me seeing double, so I put the gun down. Wade knew it wasn't still loaded.

"We're getting out of here," I told him. Annie could drive us the rest of the way. We weren't more than forty miles from the farm. The cops would be waiting there to castrate me. There was no dodging fate. I prepared myself for the consequences when the Captain at last tendered what seemed like a fairly good idea.

"We'll torch it!" he exclaimed.

"Are you insane?" Annie asked him.

"He's not crazy," I vouched.

Then the Captain said, "Dear, your husband is more mental then you realize."

But I wasn't mad. I was driven. And the only honest thing on my mind was getting out, getting home. The rest could be deliberated in the morning, possibly in front of a judge if we made it until then.

In any case, we burned it.

Flame stretched skyward into the night. It was surreal. Annie and Wade roasted marshmallows over the top of the glowing frame, singing campfire songs she'd learned in 4-H.

I was in no mood for singing. My life as I knew it was over. They'd be coming to take me away, just as Kelsey predicted. Wouldn't she be pleased? Wouldn't my mother be so proud of me then?

"What the fuck is wrong with you guys?" I asked.

They seemed perturbed at the interruption. The singing stopped as the fire died down.

Wade fed his dog in the bushes. Annie was utterly pastoral. She was always that way. It drove me mad. Had she no shame?

We were fugitives and no one seemed to care. I was just looking for a fight, feeling the full weight of responsibility, but there were no takers.

Annie helped me find a log to sit on while I collected myself. It was late and I hadn't slept for days. I fought back tears, I'll admit. The Captain stood at my side. Annie eventually joined him.

He said, "Life is just a dream, my boy."

I wished that it was. But the scent of burnt petroleum kept me lucid.

They wouldn't have to explain it all, or testify.

If worst came to worst, I decided, I'd kill myself. It's important to always have a pinch plan.

◆ ◆ ◆

I told my counselor that I was going to do it that very night.

"That would stop all their carousing," I said.

"Would it?" Marie asked.

I hadn't decided how, or at what point to end it, but after the Captain drove us back to Hazard and I exhausted all other, more endurable, remedies, including the bottle he left, I knew we weren't fooling anyone. There were no cops in the vicinity, but Guy Manchetti would want retribution. He was out there somewhere, too.

As a last resort, I tried summoning *soarta*. Inspiration. Literary greatness. But when seated at the kitchen table in front of the blank page, the adage to speak toward resolution hadn't come to me; I simply gave up searching to find it.

"How did it end up?" Marie asked.

Of course, she was curious to know; but by that time, it seemed absurd to tell her. The session was not for her entertainment or training.

Was it compulsory that I continued on?

No. I didn't think so.

She was writing something heinous about me again.

So I told her, "We slept like the dead."

Chapter 9

THEY WEREN'T ENTIRELY UNTRUE, the things I'd told my counselor.

Sure, most of it was exaggerated to some extent, for effect. It was her area of expertise to decipher, I assumed. At the core of it, there was the extremely existential problem I'd posed about the future, which continued to plague me long after I knew our session was technically complete.

We'd gone well beyond the hour and a half allotted. I don't know how far past, though it was some time before I ever glanced at the clock. By then, I felt certain that whatever obligation I had to pursue *soarta* exhaustively, including therapeutic remediation, had been satisfied for the day. Marie knew it, as well, though she never mentioned that. I believe she was too enthralled. Maybe I'd gone too far into detail. I could have summarized, but I at least knew that I had myself a good story.

It had led to my being in shackles, after all. Not the metaphorical ones I'd been discussing at length, but the cold hard steel variety. Since we were apparently continuing on, I decided to keep it interesting, including the good stuff, which I was getting to. But before I got into that, I had to lay some ground rules.

I told Marie that I didn't want her getting the wrong idea.

"About what?" she asked.

"About my will to live or lack thereof. I'm not really suicidal."

"You've mentioned it many times."

"Just so you understand that I wasn't really going to do it."

She put down her notepad. I could see by her look that this was going to be a serious point of contention, in need of immediate clarification for the official record.

I testified that it was a quintessential aspect of my nature as a fiction writer to embellish certain details in order to make a clearer point. It was for her benefit. That was the honest-to-God truth.

"What parts did you make up?" Marie asked.

"The parts that could have me involuntarily committed," I replied.

"That's what I thought," she stated bluntly, and went back to taking notes.

I reasoned we had a good enough understanding to continue on unfettered.

For the sake of time, I skipped forward to the part where I found myself in the hangman's noose.

◆ ◆ ◆

A couple days had passed since the honeymoon in Maine. Annie had just gone to see a specialist for her night terrors and lethargy, and I decided to use that time to analyze and reflect upon things. I got out my pen and notepad with the idea that I'd write down everything I remembered.

It wasn't much.

By the time I finished with the facts and translated my feeble attempt at shorthand from our first night at the cabin, I hadn't even filled up a page, so I turned my attention toward watching Dirk out the window and drinking beer.

He was wrestling with one of his cattle, trying to steer the old milker into position. He had a host of rusty tools and other implements waiting to carve her up. He'd said many times that everything on the farm had a purpose, including the cow. Rylee was Annie's favorite. She groomed her on a regular basis and spent a considerable amount of time at the udder. Even I'd drunk straight from the nipple once. It tasted just like manure smelled. But when the Jersey stopped giving milk, both of them seemed quick to abandon her. They suddenly wanted steak.

Dirk had come inside that morning, interrupting my plans to narrate in peace. He was sweating profusely in spite of the cold, having already tried fooling Rylee into volunteering for the guillotine with some grain, and then resorted to plowing her massive body out of the stall by force. When he'd succeeded, he'd then had to give chase. He described his plans for the dis-section in gory detail.

"We'll make it quick and easy," he explained.

"I can't do it," I insisted.

"Why not?" Dirk asked.

I told him I had important work to do, which could not wait. Besides that, I said, the cow and I had become far too inti-mate—not in the hillbilly way he imagined. But I'd stared deeply into her enormous black bulging eyes and seen the spirit within.

"I'm much too loyal," I explained.

With that, Dirk was gone, having called me a pussy. He decided he could handle the job easily on his own, but I could see he was mistaken. Judging by the look of it, he'd underesti-mated the old nag. Rylee fought for her pathetic, slavish life, and as I watched it all unfold, wondering why she bothered to struggle so hard.

Dirk wasn't about to give up. Nevertheless, when Rylee bucked and kicked him squarely in the face, I put my money on her. I thought I might go vegan if she prevailed. There was no stopping the farmer, though I considered trying. At one point I went for my father's gun in an attempt to stage some half-cocked intervention, but her fate was already sealed.

Dirk sprang up with a look of sheer determination, squint-ing to see through the sweat, blood, and manure that covered his face. Then he reached for his dagger and I looked away.

It was at this point I suddenly realized more of what Aishé had been trying to tell me about life, destiny, and the nature of people. We are all desperate to live and serve a purpose, whether against our own will or toward it. At the end of life is death. What happens in between, no matter what our particular stable, was *soarta*. The realization made me sick to my stomach.

I closed the blinds.

Annie had convinced me to stay. She overwhelmed me with cause, kept me soaked with liquor, and then pinned me down against the bed one of those nights. In a moment of weakness, I gave into her lustfulness. It was a rare opportunity, at least where I was involved. Then she twisted the screws farther in.

After our haymaking, I went limp integrally. That's when she said she wanted to see a doctor.

"You need to stay," she whispered, insisting I go back to work at the dealership for the health insurance.

"Are you totally insane?" I asked.

"Just for the short term," Annie promised, with the assurance that once her issues were resolved things would get better. That was *if* the matter wasn't something serious. Only then could I quit as planned.

It seemed there was always some loony reason for me to stay there. Now: hypochondria.

"You must think I'm a fool!" I said.

But Annie wasn't playing. She went for the close, handed me a cold one, and batted those pale blue eyes expectantly. Knowing my weaknesses in those regards, she asked me to focus. "I know you want what's best for me," she said.

That was the truth. Good God! She had problems. As always, they were more preeminent than mine, but I had a heart to fix them.

As a matter of fact, there were several problems.

The first one had to do with me, admittedly. I'm not proud of it. But in reality, I was no longer in the relationship for the long haul. Her need, now becoming synonymous with Stager and my personal sacrifice—immolation—had something to do with it, but that was just affirming what I thought I already knew. I let Annie believe otherwise, because I had no better plan in view besides drinking with her father nightly to dull the pain.

That said, I'd agreed to her terms in the interest of her well-being; I went back to work and did what any rational, desperate, caring person would do in my situation.

I began to canvass the realm of possibility. I resurrected the old online dating profile, made certain revisions to include the word "author" wherever it seemed most impressive. And I called Kelsey more than once to disrupt whatever courtship she might've had going, knowing fully that I would not have gotten past the whole raft guide thing if she'd answered. She never did.

I knew there'd be plenty of time for striking contingencies. Annie said the doctors had a barrage of tests planned to rule out something horrid. She obsessed about it in the meantime. I'd assured her there was nothing medical to worry about.

She had all of the best treatment at her disposal, mind you. Thanks to Paul Stager, we all had top-notch coverage, including a rider for mental debility, which he secured after the whole Peggy thing left him practically in the poorhouse. Annie was prepared to use every bit of it.

The next morning, the day of her appointment, before Dirk even had his coffee I awoke to her unconscious shrieks, babble, and another bad headache. "I can't do this!" I declared.

The exclamation startled her. Annie leapt from the bed and told me she'd been dreaming about her mother. To keep me from resignation, she said she knew there was something wrong.

"I'm not sleeping well," she told me.

"You sleep all the time!" I exclaimed. "*I'm* the one who can't sleep! Jesus! Can you blame me?"

"Rob, you slept for almost a whole day, through the entire ceremony."

"Yes, but I was drugged, goddamn it! It wasn't good sleep," I said. Not that any of my afflictions ever seemed to matter to her or warrant further examination.

Annie dismissed it.

She focused on herself, and figured her malady had everything to do with menopause.

"You're twenty-eight years old!" I pointed out.

But her mother had over-matured quickly, also, and it'd contributed to her demise. I didn't have all the scientific details, though Annie believed that cancer was generational. I wasn't about to be held responsible for her physical deterioration, even if at present I maintained that the symptoms were strictly in her head. Nevertheless, I indulged her, and got ready for work, stipulating that she exercise her right to a medical facility sooner rather than later.

And then, when I knew she was gone, I took off the blue Stager polo to write and take advantage of the opportunity without any distraction.

There was no meditative silence so long as she was around squawking about pestilence, obligations, and insurance. Even with her gone, it was the only thing I could think about, so I cracked a cold one for amnesty. It had no positive effect. By the time I finished it, my inner voice turned bitter. The page was still practically blank.

Mainly, I wanted Annie to realize that—in spite of my charity toward her and bravery during the Maine extraction— my affections had waned. Her indifference toward me there, her failure to defend me from the lesbians or abide by any of the rules of matrimony had irreparably soured me to her and her kind. Those conditions made it impossible to focus.

The anger over it blocked out any good ideas flowing through my tired brain. Whatever I wrote down, the utterance had to be profound. The words had to be great, chosen precisely for the purpose of definition and perhaps retribution, but not rage. The critics—Paul Stager, and everyone else I'd been lying to for years about my stupendous literary capacity—would tear me apart for that. Acrimony is an easy proposition, as far as manuscript goes. True love is not.

The problem vexed me for hours. What was that indescribable story I'd been mad to tell? Perhaps summarizing it exceeded my ability.

The thought of that steered me toward horrible, unthinkable, nasty thoughts.

So I put away the pen and paper. I packed up all my important belongings and had the baggage waiting to greet Annie when she came through the door. She could donate it to charity. I wasn't leaving her with a mess.

In the meantime, I went outside and saw Dirk with half of Rylee dangling from a chain attached to a tree. He was in the process of trimming the fat. So was I.

I ignored him when he asked for help. I was on a mission, with an armload of Stager uniforms bundled underneath each arm, a Marlboro pressed between my lips, and a bottle of lighter fluid. I dropped the polos in the grass and squirted them thoroughly. Then I struck a match, lit my cigarette, puffed a few times, and dropped it.

I saw my years at Stager, lying prostrate to Paul and his evil blood-sucking patrons, go up in smoke. It was a glorious sight. Even Dirk joined in the revival.

"What's going on here?" he asked.

I told him I was freeing myself from languid encapture. He scratched his head for a second.

"Life isn't fair," he replied.

"I'll miss it in some ways," I said.

"Your job?"

"No, not that!"

We'd had a lot of interesting conversations, he and I. It was all novel-worthy, not that I could think of any way to write it down.

He pondered things, warmed his hands against the glowing stack of polyester, and then said he was going to get us some wine.

He returned a minute later with two jugs, uncorked them both, and handed me one. The other he poured straight into his gullet. I followed suit. For once he had a rational topic in mind.

He said, "When Leona was diagnosed, I thought my life was over. She went bald and nothing's been good ever since. Not because of what the doctors did, or tried to do. Not because she was disfigured. Oh no! She was still a beautiful woman. The most beautiful I've ever seen, before or since. But the cancer came with a lot of obligation." The memory of it made his bloody hands tremble. He took another drink. "I was there for her. She never complained or asked for anything. But I was there. It was awful seeing her that way. I prayed, but it didn't do either one of us a damn bit of good. I thought of leaving her. Can you believe that? Not because loving her was hard, but because walking away seemed so easy."

"But you didn't leave," I said, commending him.

"I did!" he replied. "Not physically, but in every other way." It haunted him, though he'd tried exorcizing the demon with alcohol. I tried to collaborate.

"You did everything you could," I stated in between glugs. It was the best consolation I could muster at the time.

"I could have done more," Dirk replied.

He finished off his bottle just as I finished mine and headed back toward butchering the milker. I felt for the man and thought I should have offered more in the way of encouragement as he walked with the two empty jugs in hand. But nothing brilliant came to mind. He turned the corner and I thought it was the last I'd see him.

Good-bye, Dirk, I waved.

Now, getting back to my own problems, I stewed as the fire died down.

Something he'd said about Leona stuck with me. It was the part about loving being hard. It was so true and poetic; most people would never understand. But true love, however you picture it, will demand everything, and his sacrifice was wondrous. It's not at all like what you read about or watch on TV. We learned the hard way.

Before the last flame went out, I dropped my khakis to piss on the embers. They hissed at me in disapproval.

"Fuck you, Stager," I whispered. Dirk couldn't hear. He was too busy chopping through sinew. The man was more beautiful than he knew. Crazy. And more beautiful than I had realized before then.

I went back inside, found a rope, and tied it to one of the rafters he'd laid by hand. I let it dangle there in the living room while I tried to conjure up something clever and prosaic. My last words.

It was utterly important that they not come across as indignant.

TO THOSE I BLAME FOR THIS, I started out.

No, that wasn't right. I scratched it and tried again.

I then scribbled the words *LIFE IS JUST A RECURRING NIGHTMARE*, but it sounded too contrived. So I started again by scratching the name *LEE DONEGAN*, let it sit for a while, and then tore the page to shreds.

I couldn't give that bastard the satisfaction. Damned writer's block!

Next, I tied the noose, having researched the proper way to do so on the internet. I checked the inbox on my dating profile also, and looked for any messages from Kelsey, while I was at it. Upon seeing no signs of hope that I could follow, I climbed up on a chair and stuck my head inside the cord. It was scratchy and irritated my neck considerably.

Though there was no superb note to speak of my existence, I assured myself that Annie and others would get the idea when she came home to find me lifeless and strung, the way I'd always been as it pertained to their abuses. Surely they'd all get the picture when they realized that my devotion and years of servitude had resulted in my sad, tragic demise. Or would they?

There was some doubt, which was why I had a second chair placed strategically nearby, just in case I decided in some last gasping plea for acknowledgment that I'd need more assurance before signing off.

"Good-bye, world," I said.

It was good-bye to everything, including hope, love, *soarta*, my novel, raft guides, Stager, ambition, the law, the farm, fate, family, Annie, and everyone. *Hallelujah*! I prayed God would forgive me and see me through to that green felt-topped gambler's table above.

I kicked out the chair without further delay. The itching rope was driving me crazy. I felt it cinch tight across my esophagus and instantly regretted it. Suddenly, the rusted guardrail flashed into view as I was once again in communion with the infinite plow of words and wisdom that had me proclaiming there. Now I couldn't say a word. What had I done?

I quickly tried reaching my foot toward the auxiliary seat, but it was too far out of range to touch. In my desperation, I started swinging, as the whole entire narrative of what the universe itself had predestined me to scribe—including dialogue— manifested in my oxygen-starved brain. I saw the poor, pathetic note I'd attempted to leave behind in pieces on the floor. That wasn't going to be my legacy.

With each pendulum thrust, the chair and salvation grew closer. Then I touched upon it. My sneaker stuck to the worn, wooden seat like glue. I couldn't breathe at all, though I knew if I could manage to slide the piece toward me, there'd be rescue and then vindication in the form of metric composition.

At that point I gave fortuity all I had left to give. She answered in kind, as the heavy, antique bergère finally budged and lurched in my direction. I clasped my other foot around the padded armrest and drew it closer until, at last, I could finally relieve the horrid constriction.

I breathed deeply, allowed my neurons to recover, and untied the line from the ceiling in haste before the blessed composition had a chance to escape.

I wrote everything down, receiving each word like a prophet, without considering the consequence of what I'd divined. I didn't waste time with the noose—couldn't feel it, either, in my catharsis. Suddenly there were pages full, and I continued on throughout the rest of the day and night, filling them with fact and fable, drawing blurry lines between the two until I'd said everything there was to say on the subject of love being hard.

Somewhere in all my correspondence, around the time I got to telling about Dirk, I realized that genuine adulation required forfeit—*worship*, both in the literary sense that I'd fawned after and of the romantic variety. It'd turned out to be a great deal more sacrifice than I'd anticipated or hoped for.

That might've softened a better man toward Annie. She was a perfectly willing consort. I saw her as invulnerable, though; the careless, sweet, unapologetic, not sarcastic or bitter opposite of me. And I wanted her to love me back, exclusively. But did she? Was she even capable? That was really the question.

She came through the front door at that moment with a sad look upon her face. I still had the rope hanging loosely around my neck as I sat over the stack of chapters at the kitchen table. She walked past my duffel bags, set her keys on the counter, and opened the refrigerator door. Then she pulled out a couple beers, cracked them both, and started to guzzle.

I said, "Those doctors have done wonders!"

Annie started to cry.

It was awful. I'd never seen her that way, so forlorn.

I told her Rylee was in a better place. I'd seen it glistening, momentarily. It was wonderful.

"Never mind the cow," she replied.

I knew the matter was serious, so I untethered myself from the length of cord, instantly severing every transpondence that came with it. She handed me one of the beers.

"What is it?" I asked.

"You'll need to drink," she said.

There was something completely heinous troubling her. It showed in her overly impetuous attitude, the way she nervously handed me a beer, and then, when I quickly finished that, gave me another one. Annie was even keeping pace.

She asked if I was seeing someone else.

"Of course not!" I replied.

For all our escapades in the North, the uncertainty that followed, and other considerations, I'd never given her any good reason to think it. I was no sly adulterer. Despite having no solid religious code, whatever it was, that particular sin was against my very nature. Besides that, I'd seen the light, which had been revealed to me cathartically in a near suicidal contrivance. Maybe it was love. But even if it wasn't, I'd have filed for the annulment at least before moving on.

"What on earth would make you ask that?" I questioned, opening my next libation under Annie's watchful instruction.

She said a lot of things had come into focus. Didn't I know it!

It was good of me, she explained, staying dedicated to her the way that I had. She admitted Lee Donegan was a treacherous swine. The rest of it I already knew, including that she'd certainly been less than nurturing where cultivating our bondship was concerned.

"So what's got you going?" I inquired.

Annie dug deeper and looked down, studying the length of rope coiled on the kitchen floor. It didn't take her long to put it together.

"Were you just trying to kill yourself?" she asked.

It was a valid line of questioning, I thought—one better left for another day.

Then Dirk came in with a plateload of meat. He said it needed to be consumed or preserved or risk spoilage.

"Do you have any room in your freezer?" he asked.

"I'm glad you're here," Annie said.

Her father boasted, "Rylee was old and emaciated, but she sure gave off a big roast."

"Good God, man!" I replied.

Couldn't he tell that we were in the midst of some hefty revelation?

Annie threw one of her empty bottles down onto the floor. It smashed into a million pieces. Dirk jumped back, just as I did, at the sudden crash.

"Now that I have all your attention," Annie said. The room went silent. She had something important to say as she began to wipe the tears out from her eyes. I was on pins and needles, but it wasn't rapture.

Dirk sat himself on my redemption chair and placed what was left of Rylee on the counter. The whole scene was a disgusting mess. I hate reliving it.

"Go on," her father grumbled.

Annie said, "Well it's been quite a while since I've said this, but I'm grateful to you both for being here for me. I know it's not always been easy. I haven't always done the right thing. I wish I had, because now I need you more than ever."

"Oh my God, are you pregnant?" I asked.

"No," said Annie. "They think I have cancer."

Chapter 10

I TOOK ANNIE TO THE HOSPITAL the very next morning for surgery. She said the doctors recommended biopsy and excision. It was supposedly routine, but that was easy for them to say at the start of a terrifying diagnostic process to confirm what they probably knew already. I knew it too.

My heart had been in an awful state of spasm ever since Annie broke the news. I was nervous as a tick on dip day. I played it off and tried to act natural through chest-puffery, so as not to worry her even more. When we drove toward the clinic, I told her those doctors didn't know what they were in for if they thought I would hesitate to unleash Hell to keep things running smoothly. Annie smiled. Then, to keep her grinning, I let off with a steady stream of wit and sarcasm as we came through the doors until she told me to stop.

It was no laughing matter. I knew.

Perhaps in Annie's mind, some hopeful doubt still existed about the prognosis. I didn't ever say otherwise and tried to contain myself after that.

Cancer, that irrevocable scourge, was prewritten in her DNA from the day she was born. It was so unfair. She'd said so herself previously, the few times she ever spoke about what killed her mother. It was only a matter of time, she'd proffer, and I'd never believed her until then.

Now we were sitting in a shabby, supposedly private pre-operative waiting area, where you'd have thought there'd have been some sign of gratuity for all the billions those places suck from the desperate. Instead, they used the space to store medical pamphlets, which were haphazardly stacked from the worn linoleum to the water-stained ceiling.

Annie was trembling as we watched for the doctor. She gripped my hand hard and said she was feeling woozy. Her palms were sweating from nerves. I assured her everything was going to be fine.

"These people are brilliant practitioners," I said. I assumed they were.

"That's what we told Mom," she replied.

I told her those were more primitive times. Advances in sciences, therapy, and medicine since then had surely shifted the probabilities in her favor. Admittedly, I didn't know the odds. Annie never gave the morbid statistics, if she had them. She knew I didn't possess a sufficient morale to float the both of us if things got any bleaker.

Dirk couldn't bear to know the harsh reality, either. He stayed back at the farm and kept his mind focused on chores. I'd promised to stay at the hospital, though, through the entire procedure, and to be there when Annie came to.

I was beginning to have some serious concerns about the chances when the doctor sluggishly approached. He was young, clearly exhausted, and very Indian. I couldn't understand a word he said. It was not at all a confidence-inspiring greeting. He motioned for me to sit down; I was only trying to shake his hand.

"It's customary," I explained to him.

I tried grabbing his right arm, which he rudely retracted.

"Sit down!" Annie demanded, and I did abide, though not without voicing my displeasure.

Bear in mind that I was just looking out for her, trying to build rapport with the people in charge. I had no particular disdain for foreigners in general. I am not prejudiced in the slightest. It was only that I assumed the procedure about to be performed required a great deal of deftness and communication. This particular man was clearly lacking in both. I said as much, and that I was simply trying to be cordial with the man when he rebuked my honest initiatives. Now he was visibly agitated, and dear sweet Annie's life was about to be laid in his wringing hands.

"Could we have a moment to discuss liabilities?" he asked.

"I was just getting there!" I told him.

He was about to talk about the odds when Annie quickly cut him off.

"I don't want to know them," she said.

Thank God.

Seconds later, it was time. The doctor yawned. He coaxed her on. The thought of them slicing Annie made me sick. Poor girl. She kissed me good-bye sweetly and went along willingly, in spite of my trepidation.

"Don't go," I blurted out, but the two continued off in the direction of a surgical theater—so much for solemn advocacy. I told her not to worry, though. "I'll be right here," I assured her, making certain the surgeon heard me also, to keep him accountable and focused on the task.

I followed them down the hall just as far as the orderlies would allow. When one of them stopped me, I informed her about the series of catastrophic disasters that would befall the whole complex facility if the second-rate import didn't do his job.

"You sound a lot like a terrorist," she said.

"He better turn out to be somehow enlightened," I warned.

The orderly rolled her eyes. She obviously had no idea about my propensity for destruction, intentional or otherwise. For the most part, it came naturally. My instincts told me that Annie, in spite of her numerous shortfalls, deserved a grand cataclysmic gesture should she perish under the knife. That was love, not rage. She was, if nothing else, a vernal babe in the woods who'd tolerated my eccentricities better than most. If ever there was a legitimate, opportune case provided by the cosmos to utilize, and therefore heroically justify, my particular set of skills in the way of spontaneous calamity, this was it.

I returned to the waiting room with the intention of staying vigilant. There I found an unfamiliar woman. She was a diminutive elder-librarian cat-lady type who'd occupied no less than one half of the four chairs provided. Her assortment of snacks and other personal effects covered the rest.

"Can I help you?" I asked.

"Oh, I just need some peace and quiet," she replied.

"You're aware this room is private?"

"Yes, it's wonderful," she answered, appearing to settle in for the duration. She'd mentioned her name but I quickly forgot it. She explained that the communal waiting area was overcrowded and much too loud for reading. She set a Stephen King novel aside as she cleared a spot for me to sit. "Pretzels?"

"No, thank you."

"Suit yourself," she said, munching. "Do you like to read?"

I told her that I'd read a great many books, most of which were probably over her head, and the lady recoiled, mouth agape, with her loose jowls flapping. She looked like a Betty to me. "I'm a writer," I explained, and Betty was quick to pardon.

She was enthralled, actually, from that point on. I could hardly get a word in if I'd wanted to. The woman was a *bona fide* stalker. Betty called herself that, because she was obsessed with an assortment of writers.

"Have you ever been to Maine?" she asked. I nodded. "And how did you find it?"

"Like a nightmare," I replied.

"Exactly!"

Betty said she'd been to Stephen King's personal residence on West Broadway Street in Bangor. That wasn't part of any tour, she pointed out, and said the cops charged her with trespassing more than once.

I couldn't help but think her affections were wasted on the man. He wrote such twisted drivel. I thought of giving her my address for future reference, but then she claimed to have the framed citations to prove she was capable of acting out her wildest fantasies—and because I believed her, having read *Misery* once out of boredom, I decided it was best not to offer any specifics.

"What do you write about?" Betty asked.

"The truth," I replied.

She said she preferred fiction. Some people call it that. Lucky for me, Betty favored suspense and the supernatural. "And romance novels!" she added in exaltation.

"That sappy garbage?"

"How would you know, if you've never read it?"

I didn't have to. "Just look at the covers," I said.

They didn't resemble any form of mateship that I'd ever experienced. There's always too much skin and never any indication of the years of suffering involved. How authentic or entertaining could the story be if the models didn't both have huge bags under their eyes and flab from all the beer? Romance, my ass.

At this point I heard a commotion coming from down the hall. Surely Annie's procedure hadn't even begun. I stood to investigate and saw the Indian face-to-face with a cop, desperately trying to communicate something to the officer. The cop shook his head. He couldn't understand a word. Then I heard the doctor say my name. He ratted me out and quickly gave away my position, pointing back down the corridor. The officer interpreted *that*.

He looked and we made eye contact; then he came charging.

I didn't resist. That would've only made matters worse. He ordered me to hold still or be flogged into submission. I put my hands up in surrender. Betty seemed powerfully enthralled. When he slapped the cuffs on she let out a gasp.

"Where are you taking him?" she asked.

"To jail," the officer responded.

"For what?" the woman pressed.

The turncoat Indian stood by with his arms crossed.

"Isn't this some sort of HIPAA violation?" I interjected.

"Quiet, you!" the cop chastened. He proceeded to outline the allegations for all of us, which included automotive theft and the kidnapping of a raft guide—Lee Donegan—and leaving him for dead, defenseless in the North Woods.

That weasel was anything but defenseless.

"I wasn't the driver," I tried explaining, but the lawman was not having it. "I'm the victim here," I shouted as he ratcheted the cuffs down tightly. "In more ways than one!"

"Tell it to the judge," he said.

"Oh, how clichéd," was my response. But I assured him— and Betty—that I would tell everything one way or another.

In the meantime, Annie was in the midst of a life-and-death struggle of her own. I felt helpless and devoid of any self-interest or shame as the officer dragged me away. I asked Betty to please give Annie a ride home and inform my sickly wife, by way of the attendant, about my current disposition.

"What should I say?" she asked.

The cop tried muzzling me then, with one of his hairy paws covering my nose and mouth. I couldn't respond or breathe, so I nipped him slightly with my two front teeth. He released his grip and added that to the charges, and I shouted that I was getting the rap for everything—not guilty except by peripheral association to the treacherous river scum.

Then he clubbed me upside the head for the apology and forced me out, leaving Annie there to fend for herself. I didn't say a word in my defense after that. It was clear he was not a compassionate, reasonable confidant.

At the prison, he said the regular holding cells were too full.

"Bullshit!" I exclaimed, wise enough to recognize an inside slant job when I saw one.

He picked my pockets clean for evidentiary purposes, snatched my phone, and fumbled through the contents before handing everything over to the warden. I knew what he was searching for. Just being luckless didn't make me stupid enough to keep the limo keys on or about my person. People could get the wrong idea.

I figured all along that I'd have to account for and explain, in some kind of official capacity, the desperate measures I resorted to as a means of survival up north. Hard time in the slammer was the worst-case scenario. The task of indicting preponderances was daunting enough without scars and irrefutable evidence there to muddy the waters. It wasn't pure or simple—life just isn't. But I was no outlaw, the way I saw it, unless moxie was a crime.

Next he showed me to my cage, where I would become acquainted with my cellmate, Terry "The Cannibal." The cop called him that and didn't explain the charges to my satisfaction before slamming the door shut behind me.

Now I'd been fed to the savages. What kind of Podunk penitentiary system had I gotten myself into?

Hazard. That's the kind.

I sensed The Cannibal's hungry eyes staring at me in anticipation from behind. There was no rationalizing this, no escape, and no adequate metaphor to describe the feeling.

By that time I assumed Annie was likely drugged up in the recovery room, hooked into machines, and guessing about what happened to me. It seemed now she'd never know the whole story. With all the morphine, perhaps she'd be indifferent.

Having already resigned myself to the circumstance on my end, the only thing that mattered to me was her condition. I yelled through the bars that I was entitled to a phone call, at least.

"We might be feral, but even animals have rights!" I shouted madly.

Some of the guards came walking over at this juncture out of curiosity. I recognized one of them. It was Kelsey's boyfriend,

Diego, whom I met at Aaron's wedding. He felt safe on the other side of the bars, laughing with the others at my state of despair, because they were mindless barbarians with a blood-thirst for spectacle and oppression.

He said, "If there's anything we can do to make your stay more enjoyable, please let us know."

"I want my phone call," I told him. I demanded it. I couldn't speak for those other condemned mongrels, but I was innocent.

Diego raised an eyebrow and cocked his head, grinning. "What an unfortunate circumstance," he said, though he thoroughly enjoyed it.

I witnessed him fist bump another officer. That was a rather incendiary gesture, so I told him he was a hopeless captive too.

That struck a chord.

At that point Diego lost his edge and the condescending smirk went along with it.

"What do you mean by that?" he asked in a flurried mix of Spanish and English.

I said, "That biological clock is always ticking."

Then he threw a fit, howling over what he thought about my attitude. He shook the cage with his fists and threatened to chew my head off. The other guards came stampeding after and kept him in restraint.

"There'll be no mastication here—besides yours!" I swore, vowing to testify to the judge and others about his short temper, lack of professionalism, and clear conflict of interest.

This incited him further into bestial rage, his fundamental state. Diego now showed his chipped, yellow, cracked teeth and incisors capped with gold. He threw a logbook at me. It was quite a lame display. All the other inmates had seen it and began to threaten mutiny as the guards withdrew to the sound of their insidious clanging.

"You won't survive a night in here, you crazy son of a bitch!" Diego roared, revealing, as his handlers swept him off, that my cellie was chosen especially for me.

The Cannibal kept to himself, in his corner, throughout the exchange. I slowly turned to face him.

He'd surely witnessed the acclimation process before, perhaps a hundred times, during his time in captivity. What made my situation different, he said eventually, was that I'd managed to get under the guard's skin.

"It's a gift I have," I told him. I admitted that I had many in the same vein.

That seemed to break the ice. The Cannibal laughed. He said he hadn't smiled so much in more than thirty years. Terry was a lifelong criminal, incarcerated on and off since the age of thirteen when he first developed a taste, out of some necessity, for human flesh.

"The whole system is an unpardonable nightmare," he said.

Judging by that statement and his confines—which I surveyed thoroughly—I wondered why he'd had any reason since then to ever smile at all. The conditions were enough to make anyone depressed, gray, and deplorable. There wasn't so much as a writer's table to scribe handwritten notes in crayon to anyone on the outside who cared enough to read them.

We had a pot to piss in, two pathetic cots, and an inordinately large television, which he said he barely watched except during football season. There was never anything good on. The giant, ancient tube took up a fifth of the living space. It was insane.

Besides that, there were no windows to spur imagination— just three walls and a partly obstructed view through bars of the institution, the staff, and the farthest thing from any rational attempt at rehabilitation that I'd ever seen.

"You must be a saint," I told Terry, "because I'd have hung myself with bedsheets like fifteen years ago."

"I'm no saint," he responded quickly, but without lurching for my throat, so I knew that we had something of a constitution there to build upon.

I settled down some, though ever aware of the fact that any incarcerated person with a nickname like Cannibal was a certified lunatic. I didn't ask about his glory days, figuring the moniker told me all I needed to know or cared to understand. Outside of that, he wasn't so bad, though the stigma lingered. I reasoned it was best to keep him laughing.

I saw him lick his lips more than once. That's a fact. I speculated that he was, perhaps, sizing me up, or the capacity and disposition of his ravenous, reputedly indiscriminate appetite. There was a lot to consider.

In an effort to bait him off my scent, I asked when the miscreants served lunch.

"They just did," Terry replied.

"I'm sorry to have missed it," I said nervously.

And The Cannibal answered, "Oh, you didn't."

Next came a very tense few moments, where I saw my life flash before my eyes. That was not cliché.

Terry literally pulled a shank that he'd kept hidden from his keepers behind the toilet. It was obviously a prized possession. The knife was made of steel—part of the bedframe, I assumed. He held up the blade so I could see the quality of workmanship. It was spectacularly honed. I said as much, just catching a glimpse of myself in the high polished metal, as he then turned toward the two platters of prison fare and began to carve.

I breathed a sigh of relief when the hungry loon began to pray over the slop.

"Dear Heavenly Father," he began. I lowered my head as he continued on, out of reverence and respect, but didn't take my eyes off him even for a split second.

Later, he complained about the quality of protein on offer as we chowed down. I tried to relate. "It's like *ding-ding*," I said, explaining the origin and stipulating that without his shiv, we'd have never gotten through it. Terry swelled with pride. He even carved my desiccated portion for me so I wouldn't choke. It was a surprisingly kind, selfless gesture for a man of his proclivity. While he sawed, he spoke about his plans to travel the world if he ever got paroled.

I told him one place was as horrible as any other, present accommodations excluded.

"That's not true," he said.

"Have you ever been to Maine?"

"No, never."

"Well, strike it from your list."

Terry nodded as he chewed and said, "I don't think I'll be going to South India either."

We were gnawing exhaustively when the full weight of reality and all my transgressions returned. I'd wanted to see Las Vegas. It had a certain runaway allure. I wondered, would it still, after doing five to ten? The Cannibal offered hope in that regard. He brought up Sin City before I even had a chance to mention it. The Golden Nugget was the first of his planned destinations.

"It's beautiful," he said. "Not at all like those commercial monstrosities farther down Las Vegas Boulevard. And the beer there flows like sink water."

I did a little dance and Terry laughed.

He said he got picked up by security while at the old casino's grand nine-dollar buffet, where he spent much of his time sampling delicacies.

My mouth watered at the thought of a smorgasbord. "Are those places any good?" I asked.

"I wouldn't know," Terry replied. "But a host of porky tourists seemed to think so."

"I see," I replied, coughing. My mouth suddenly went dry.

Terry thought I was choking, so he quickly offered his blade. I flinched.

I told him it was just nerves, and possibly withdrawal. I hadn't had a drink in almost twenty-four hours.

"Do you have any homemade alcohol?" I asked. I didn't know what to call it. Hooch?

He said he didn't, thought a little while, and then politely offered me one of his prescribed antipsychotic pills. The guards administered those, but he regularly fooled them to stay alert, he explained. After concealing the downers underneath his tongue, he spat out the half dissolved remainder and kept a stockpile in storage for just such an occasion.

"How generous," I replied. But seeing the yellow congealed pile he offered, I graciously passed.

The other convicts got insanely drunk off toilet wine, he informed me, but that was on them if they, or I, were interested in drinking shit. Terry paused, and I assured him that I wasn't.

Right away I sharply regained focus and started plotting a course out of there, in my mind, toward acquittal. Terry offered a lot in the way of hospitality and fodder for the book I now felt capable of writing. But fecal alcohol was where I drew the line.

Besides that stomach-churning invention, there was Annie, who surely needed me. The thought of her in the hospital alone, in the clutches of disease and the insubordinate, bush-league doctors without adequate representation, made me gag. It wasn't the *ding-ding*.

Terry offered water from the tap, but it was already too late.

"What are you, bulimic?" he asked as I puked.

I told him there was no amount of societal pressure that could keep me there. I was already going stir-crazy, just a few hours in, as The Cannibal chewed on gristle. The smell of vomit didn't faze him.

Every so often he'd thrust the shank in my direction. Each time, it caused me to lurch back in my chair, though it was only for my use. I said I'd lost my appetite. The Cannibal had not lost his; he wolfed down what was left on my tray, then mopped the floor with a bedsheet, throwing the soiled linen out for the guards to retrieve later.

For my first time in the clink, he surmised, I wasn't doing so bad. He told me things would get easier.

"What do you mean?" I mumbled, now retching with dry heaves.

"It takes time and we've got plenty," he replied.

The bastard had me pegged for common jailbird trash! I told him he was wrong. I informed him of my stock. "My father is a retired cop!" I exclaimed.

Terry told me to quiet down. "That sort of revelation could get you killed in here!"

I lowered my voice. He was right. I was out of my depth in there, for sure. But I was not the kind of degenerate garbage he was used to preaching to. I had tenure at the car dealership, where I threw my weight around freely, and a few good wives who'd have supported every claim.

"And what would they think about you *now*?" he inquired.

It was a reasonable assertion, the kind that did warrant further examination under the circumstances. I gave him that, but it was all I could offer the charlatan when he asked if I'd ever read the Good Book.

He said he started his spiritual journey while doing time in Nevada. The jury eventually acquitted him there. They couldn't prove anything. That was a miracle! He'd then headed east, hitching, to take in the whole of America, and happened to stumble into Hazard. He mentioned Gravity Hill. I told him I'd been there too. The place was a strange and obscure bit of local folklore—not truly physics-defying, but an optical illusion on private property.

But Terry didn't see it that way. There he'd lost control of his equilibrium, fallen, and log-rolled upwards. He considered the phenomenon sacred proof of God, telling him he was backward for his wicked tendencies, and that the whole world was a woefully wrong, illogical place, completely upside down. He decided to give up the cannibalism thing and attempted to set up camp on the holy site, but the Hazard police showed up while he was negotiating with the owners for continuous access.

"Damn muskers," I said in a feeble attempt at solidarity.

Terry shook his head. "They didn't know the half of it." Despite his plans for personal improvement, I'm sure he'd have enjoyed a murderous barbecue that night, except the cops promptly incarcerated him for unlawful invasion. He quickly pled guilty, considering penance. He licked his lips again— good God! Then he said, "Six months ago, I'd have swallowed someone so weak and tasty as you. But that's not the way."

I gulped the last bit of gravy-laden slop still stuck in my teeth. It was terrible. No wonder the man turned cannibalistic after years spent in jail eating like this. How he stayed on the wagon at that moment was a mystery—not that I was questioning it or contemplating headhunting, but for the first time, I sympathized with him. It was unimaginable, but I did. So I entertained what he had to say—there was no other contrivance.

He told me that God was the author of all mankind.

"I'm a writer too," I affirmed.

"Then you're in very good company."

I was hesitant to say the kind of things I chose to write on, so when he asked, I said simply, in an effort to summarize, that it was all about the unadulterated truth and hopeful adoration.

He said, "Now these three remain: faith, hope, and love." It was a quote from the Bible. "But the greatest of these is love."

I'd received the message before in church the few times I went, but never had I heard it recited so authentically, or so eloquently spoken. The Cannibal should have been a pastor. Terry was even thankful for the goulash. I reasoned that any man grateful for that unpalatable nightmare was either crazy or enlightened. He was clearly no saint, and so, erring on the side of caution, I decided to drop the subject. But The Cannibal was just getting around to making his devout impression.

He asked if I was a religious man. Reluctantly, I said I wasn't, strictly.

"That's good," he replied. "Religion is a lie, one big scam. God is another thing altogether."

It was starting to become clear to me that he was right. It seemed everyone I met had something to say on the subject of divinity. Most of them were insane, but what did that matter to me or the universe, as far as genuine counsel and prophecy was concerned? I needed it more than anyone to stay on course, especially if Aishé was right about what she foresaw.

Even in my stark, gray, seasick sobriety, I knew that she was. I pictured her out there somewhere, telling me to hang on. These were the falls, the ultimate test of my commitment to *soarta* and Annie. I was just about going over the edge when The Cannibal injected his thoughts.

He asked me to pray with him, and I did, lowering my head in total submission to the cull as the fear of impending consequence, contract, debt, and accountability swept across, pounding every coherent thought I had into oblivion. Terry was asking all of Babylon to bribe the judge.

"May God's will be done," he said as I was shaking.

Then all the shuddering stopped. I knew at this point that I was in free fall.

When I opened my eyes I saw the farm in spring—not the cell, not a crystal casino, but Annie and fields of verdant green. Rylee wasn't in her pen, so I knew it wasn't Heaven.

Annie motioned for me to follow her to a familiar hillside where we often watched through binoculars as Walmart patrons stumbled in the parking lot down below. They were all drunk by noon. We were drinking beer ourselves, all the while laughing hysterically like we were exceptional. That was the Cotner way. She was bald, but just as beautiful as ever. I guzzled a cold, frothy, glorious lager.

She said, "Just don't pee on my pumpkins," which was a precocious, unusual reference, I'll admit. But that's what she said in my vision.

I took it as another indecipherable sign. They were everywhere.

Chapter 11

TERRY CURLED UP IN HIS COT after the guards made their final round that night. He had their routines down to a science. He informed me when the last one passed that they'd be back with reinforcements at dawn to drag me in front of a judge. That was an all-important hearing, he assured me, not to be underestimated. I knew. My future hung in the balance.

There was no telling what time it was, but before long everyone was slumbering. I knew by the sound of snoring, which grew steadily in volume until it was impossible to differentiate one snort from another. It became a unified, sustained, echoing growl that lasted for hours and told of unspeakable heartache and dreams that would never come true.

I couldn't sleep.

Looking back, I know I needed that time to put some things into perspective. Mainly, I thought of Annie. I hadn't yet gotten a chance to make my phone call, but I thought about calling her and saying that I was prepared to forgive the lies she'd told and the things she omitted. I'd tell her that I read her journal; it wasn't the crime of the century—hers or mine. Next I'd ask her to contact a decent attorney, from her hospital bed, before morning.

The opportunity came much sooner than I expected.

I heard keys jangling—the sound of an approaching guard. It was Diego who appeared. He stood at the gate with a finger pressed to his lips.

I stayed quiet as he motioned me out, without handcuffs, and gently latched the door behind me. No one stirred. He led me down the hall, past the other cells and sleeping mongrels, to an office with a telephone.

Now I had two choices. He said it was 5:30 a.m. I could call Annie and wake her, possibly sending her into cardiac arrest, or put out an SOS to try and reach someone else—someone who was more adept at handling these kinds of situations with the long-term big picture in mind. I knew exactly who, but not how to reach Wade Balshi. He had no phone. Smoke signals would've worked better. But I knew that if I succeeded he could summon the Devil himself, if necessary, in my defense. It was not a simple matter of priority, and we didn't have all morning.

Diego tapped his finger on the desk while I decided. "One call," he whispered.

I picked up the receiver and dialed. On the other end, Aaron Turner answered.

"Don't hang up!" I exclaimed.

"Quiet down!" Diego commanded.

Aaron spoke. "Who is this?"

"It's me, goddamn it!"

"Rob?"

"Yes!" I whispered as Diego shut the office door.

"Where are you?" Aaron asked.

"Never mind that."

"Do you know what time it is?"

"Yes. Yes. Would you let me speak?"

In the background I heard Cynthia going ballistic. She was going to have to take one for the team, just as I had for their indiscretions. I told Aaron to remind her of that.

"Where have you been?" he asked.

I said, "You need to find the Captain."

"Who?"

"Wade Balshi."

"That fucking nut? What for?"

"You need to drive there. He has no phone," I explained.

Aaron said, "I thought he was in jail."

"No, he isn't—that's just the point!"

"Of what?"

I gave Aaron the directions. "Don't let the signage scare you," I insisted. "He's a great guy, just like you remember him."

"I remember him being totally crazy."

"Tell Wade I need his lawyer."

"For what?"

"Never mind that. Tell him it's urgent. Tell him to meet me at the Carbon County Courthouse. It has to do with the charred limousine. He'll understand."

Aaron paused for a moment. "Are you drunk?" he asked.

I promised him that I hadn't had a single drop.

When he hung up the phone, I wasn't sure if he'd come through. Aaron was not the most reliable salesman I'd ever met.

Diego snatched the receiver from my ear after hearing the dial tone from across the quiet room. "All done," he stated bluntly.

I told him, "I think we got disconnected."

"Nice try," he replied.

And so I was face to face with the uniformed ancillary of my first attempt at committed love. There were noticeable bags underneath each of his tired eyes. I felt for him.

"How is she?" I asked.

"You should know," Diego replied.

I recoiled. "What do you mean?"

"Oh, cut the shit, man. I know that you've been calling Kelsey."

For a moment I thought of denying it. But the truth rolled off my tongue. It was kind of a revelation. "She's never answered," I admitted.

"You're joking, right?" he asked. "She talks about you all the time!"

My heart swelled, which was fascinating, because through all my lovesick tribulation, I'd come to realize that I hated the woman down to her very narrow, self-centered core. Clearly, she had done some damage to Diego. He was jealous, possessive, and paranoid—just the way she wanted him to be. I could've illuminated the guy on everything, but then again, who was I to make his head spin when he was only trying to bury the hatchet?

"She's pregnant," he revealed.

"Oh shit! I mean, congratulations," I said.

He took it in stride. "She wants to name him Patrick."

And that is *my* middle name. I didn't tell him; not because I feared for my mortal soul— though I did—but because I suddenly hoped against all odds that he might find a way to love the child and not see it solely as an indissoluble link to Kelsey, which we both knew it was. We were all kindred now, whether Diego knew it or not.

It brought me a strange sense of peace knowing that destiny was arduously unfolding, day by day, just as it should.

"That's a great name," I assured him.

"Are you sure?" he asked.

"Yes, absolutely!" I replied. "Don't change it!"

Then Diego straightened himself, smoothed out the wrinkles from his uniform, and presented the cuffs.

"I'm sorry I have to do this," he said.

I told him I understood and offered my wrists, without objection, as consolation. He ratcheted them on loosely so that I could've escaped if I wanted to. But there comes a time of reckoning, when all things under the sun must be resolved. I knew no matter how hard I tried resisting in that moment, the time was now.

He led me back down the corridor past Terry, who was still asleep. We entered the halls of justice. The judge already sat at his throne. Diego left me at the door in the hands of the bailiff.

"Just be honest," he whispered.

I nodded and the process got underway.

First I watched as another man broke down in the courtroom after being sentenced to three years of hard time. There was a considerable docket that day, an inordinate waiting period—purgatory, as it were—before stepping forward to the pulpit and pleading your case to the state of Pennsylvania, its citizenry, and the elected executioner.

That man was the honorable Claude Chrism. He was an old-school, barrel-chested coal cracker—the kind found in pockets all the way from Appalachia to Carbon County. He chastised the dark-skinned defendant at length about his crime, which was theft by deception. The convict had done a pitiful explanatory job. His narrative was weak. I'd heard enough of it, and so had Claude.

"Come on, come on!" the judge shouted at the bailiff, motioning for him to remove the man and bring forward another inmate.

Next was a pathetic businessman cheat who said the charges against him were unfounded.

"What evidence have you?" said the judge.

The fool didn't have a shred, or a word to say, except that all his employees collectively, in an attempt to undermine his profits, had conspired against him. "*They* were the greedy ones," he proclaimed.

"I believe you," said the judge.

The man seemed relieved. Then he jumped when Claude slammed his gavel. "All people are greedy!" he proclaimed. "Especially the business types." His court date was set.

Lastly, there was a pursuant case. Mine was next. Theirs had to do with a civil litigation between a husband and wife.

She stepped warily to the stand and said her husband had taken every cent of her life inheritance and spent it, all while committing the most hideous act of adultery. Her husband protested.

He called her a lying whore. Their matter was clearly irreconcilable. He not only lacked decorum and sensitivity, but also contrition. The judge clearly knew him. The defendant addressed the court on a first-name basis, and Claude entertained his totally inaccurate and incomplete testimony about sacrifice and what the offender called "undying love."

The bastard cheated on her!

If I thought I had a shot in Hell in terms of legal counsel, I'd have objected personally right then to his fraudulency, and testified under oath that no manner of genuine endearment would result in gratuitous fornication. But I had my own problems.

Then the judge smacked his gavel in favor of the man. Claude was a crooked phony, too, and the woman walked away in tears.

I knew what I was in for as I took my turn in line. Small-town cronyism left a lot to be desired, and suddenly I was standing on the wrong side of the law. Behind me there were a hundred sniveling dogs with their stories to tell. I was sworn in. The judge's gavel banged, and I was about to speak.

Then, right on cue, the doors of fortuity opened. It was an educated clown in a zoot suit, replete with a red bowtie, who rushed into the chamber saying, "Hold everything!"

The judge cracked his stick repeatedly, but the man appeared undeterred.

He announced himself as the one and only Jim Boygos. I assumed this was my lawyer by the way he sidled up, brought out a host of miscellaneous unrelated papers, and began to recite the Constitution. The bailiff tried to restrain him, but my attorney resisted. He knew his rights. "As the fully retained, legally appointed, council of . . . " He quietly asked for my name; I whispered it in his ear. " . . . one Robert Wildhide, I compel you to drop all charges!" he said.

The courtroom fell silent. Members of the gallery craned their necks to get a better look at the spectacle as the man adjusted his collar and prepared to fearlessly spell out the exculpatory facts that would stifle even the contemptible Claude. This was a small miracle in a tiny, insignificant magisterial hall. Never before had I witnessed such a welcomed, illegitimate sight as that.

My attorney spun around as if suspended in air, now playing to the crowd, claiming he had irrefutable proof and precedence in the matter concerning the court.

"Go on," said the judge.

A second later, Jim requested a sidebar. Chrism rolled his eyes. The simple fact was that my attorney knew nothing, whatsoever, about the case at hand. He quickly turned to me.

"Give me something," he said.

The only thing I could think of saying was that Annie, my young wife, was afflicted with cancer in the hospital and in dire need. I didn't know her condition, but unless they wanted me to incite a chain gang of miscreants to rush the pulpit, I had to find a way to get back home. "Please," I begged my attorney. I was innocent.

By then the judge was getting annoyed. Just to get through the scheduled cases in time for lunch, and so as not to encourage any more of Jim's theatrics, he entertained a motion. They spoke on the side of the ornately carved mahogany bench. At one point, Claude threw his arms up. He seemed angry. I thought it was all over. Then Jim returned to the hot seat with me, winking as he came.

The judge said, "Mr. Wildhide, a Lee Donegan claims that you are on the brink of divorce, in the midst of a psychotic meltdown. Is that true?"

My attorney motioned for me to speak. I put my lips to the microphone and said "Absolutely not!"

The congregation waited in anticipation.

"Are you a reliable petitioner?"

"I believe so," I responded.

"Either you are, or you aren't," said Claude.

I told him that I was.

He deliberated while my attorney started elbowing. Claude looked out over a sea of the condemned, checked his watch, and rubbed his enormous belly. He called the prosecutor over to strategize. Moments later, they'd obviously reached some kind of agreement.

The judge eventually asked, "Is your permanent, fixed address 100 Cotner Road in Hazard, Pennsylvania?"

I gulped noticeably with my throat against the microphone as my attorney gasped. The judge reminded me that I was under oath. I'd hesitated too long for an honest answer. The congregation held their collective breath.

"I have a problem with indelible commitment sir, but I'm very good at it," I replied, finally.

The judge sternly answered, "This is not a counselor's office, sir. This is a court of law; please do not tempt my leniency— though that brings me to a bright idea." Then he banged his gavel one last time. He said, "In light of all circumstances, I sentence you to a year of special probation, barring any new evidence, to be spent monitored by anklet at the aforementioned residence."

He stipulated that I seek out some form of licensed counseling during that time, or forfeit my award and face a fickle, mindless jury of my peers.

My attorney raised his hands in victory. "You win!" he exclaimed.

But I wasn't yet convinced.

The odds of finding actual redemption in this world are one in a million. They're worse than facing Claude Chrism before noon with a thirty-foot pile of evidence smoldering just a few miles north. I have never considered myself to be a lucky man, but when the bailiff came over to take the cuffs off, I didn't argue.

I believed then, and now, that I was in the hands of fate. We all are. When you realize that, it speaks to you in ways you'd never anticipate. In my case, it corralled me ever onwards toward the place I was supposed to be. That's hard to believe, but it's true.

The bailiff swept me off. He said he was taking me home.

I accepted the verdict. By then, I'd have gone back there anyways to be with Annie, and not just because I seriously doubted The Cannibal's resolve. So it was no punishment, though my attorney was still arguing with the judge as we left, rubbing our triumph in his face. I never had a chance to thank him as my focus returned to husbandry and the rest of what destiny, God, the universe—or whatever *soarta* was calling herself in those days—had to say.

The moment I got discharged and received my phone I called the hospital for an update. The nurse said Annie was gone. My heart stopped.

"What do you mean?" I asked.

The nurse said, "Her father picked her up just a few minutes ago." She spoke very highly of Annie. "What a sweet girl, so tenacious!"

"Oh, yes," I said, agreeing.

My blood flow returned as she said the surgery went tremendously. Annie bounced right back in the recovery room and had them scrambling to get her out of there so she could get back to the farm to be with me.

It took another hour getting there the way that bailiff drove. I tried calling ahead several times, but to no avail.

"Hurry up, man," I said to him.

But the bailiff didn't abide. It was especially cold that day, even by central Pennsylvania standards. He peered through ice on the windshield and cranked the defroster, mentioning that the whole global warming concept was pure conspiracy. I didn't bother to argue. Then, when the obstruction melted, instead of flooring it, he started in with bland conversation. "So you're in car sales," he said. He'd read about it somewhere in the file.

"Not for long," I told him, explaining the outlook, Paul Stager's piety, and my contempt.

"That's too bad," he answered, because he was looking for a good deal on a Suburban. He needed something humongous for all the kids he had, and the rest he was planning on having.

I mostly blocked him out after that.

Aaron Turner became the general manager of the dealership. Paul fired me a day later when the whole thing hit the papers, for supposedly disgracing the reputation of car salespeople everywhere. I laughed hysterically over the phone. Then Paul offered to pay my health insurance for three months in lieu of severance when I promised to burn his business down if he didn't. It was a very brief, straightforward negotiation.

On my way back home to the farm after the hearing, I got a phone call from my attorney. He said all charges were going to be dropped.

"Hallelujah!" I shouted.

"It was no miracle," he said, at least not for the decedent.

Evidently, some important new evidence had already manifested. The key witness, Lee Donegan, had gotten too drunk on a float trip down the Lehigh River. He drowned and his body was never recovered. But the local cops investigating inadvertently discovered a great deal of pharmaceutical proof, corroborating most of my story and contradicting his. The state wanted nothing to do with it after that.

In a sense, I'd gotten almost everything I wished for, through trial and experience, including my emancipation from slavery at Stager, the story for my book, and the unfortunate but righteous sense of vengeful satisfaction that came from knowing Lee Donegan got what he had coming to him.

And Annie was waiting for me at home.

Those last few miles down Cotner Road were no parley. At that point I could have told the bailiff to take me anywhere. I found quite a few psychos in my dating profile that messaged during my stint, apparently impressed by my claims at authorship. Some of them were quite come-hither, in exotic locales, but I didn't say a word. What did they know about maxim or truth?

The bailiff turned up the drive. I saw the house made of fieldstone, Rylee's blood-soaked pen, and Annie bundled up with layers, sitting on the front porch in bandages with a case of Yuengling beer at her side. I remained silent.

He threw the van in park and grabbed a clipboard and the ankle bracelet as I confessed what I'd been dying to say for the last twenty miles.

"I'm a free man," I declared.

The bailiff stood in disbelief.

I told him it was the truth. He called to confirm. "Must be your lucky day," he said flippantly. Then he slowly retreated, put the monitor back in its case, and hopped in the van.

I laughed. It wasn't luck. "*Soarta* is a cold, calculating bitch," I joked.

But he didn't even crack a smile, and seemed altogether perplexed. I didn't have the time to explain it.

Annie stepped down from the porch as the bailiff drove off. We stood at the crossroads of where presage, possibility, and real life actually converged. I embraced the moment and hugged her as she handed me a cold one.

I said, "It's been a hell of a week."

Annie replied that she couldn't wait to tell me more.

We walked slowly from there, through the yard and up the adjacent field toward the highest point in all of Carbon County.

The buzzards were literally circling in formation far below us. The sun was setting over Hazard. It was a glorious sight. We gazed for a long time, just to soak it all in. Annie knew that I loved her. I didn't have to say it. And neither did she.

"Are you doing okay?" I asked.

"Yes," Annie replied. "Are you?"

I ran my fingers through her long blonde hair. She still had it then. I said, "I've never been better."

From there, we could see at least a thousand miles in every direction. The whole world was just as cold and empty as it ever was, but for now it appeared a more tolerable proposition. Annie threw her arms around me and squeezed tightly with her broad, hay-hauling shoulders until all of the blood rushed out of my veins, constricting straight into my beating heart. I squeezed her back, careful to avoid the incision.

We stayed that way for a little while. It felt like rapture. Then we turned, shivering, to watch the last light fade behind a distant mountain. There was only the Walmart store now, glistening in the twilight maybe five miles south. We headed back down toward the farmhouse to get warm, but I prayed those patrons—who probably never read books, or couldn't—might one day have the capacity to perceive what I experienced now.

♦ ♦ ♦

"Love?" my counselor prodded. She'd stopped taking notes altogether at this point.

"True love, yes."

Marie leaned into the next question. "And you don't equate any of that with imbalance, insecurity, and alcohol? I mean, Robert, what you're describing to me here, and throughout the story you've told me, isn't completely rational or healthy in any clinical sense."

"Of course not," I replied, and left it at that.

What I needed to know was how far along to let it sweep me. It was clear she had no insight to offer, and not enough life experience to inform her sterile, skeptical understanding of the things I'd said. Someday, perhaps, with the proper motivation, she would—and the fall would completely wreck her. If she was lucky.

♦ ♦ ♦

Stumbling down that hillside in the dark, Annie revealed that she was going to start chemotherapy very soon. It was a bitter-sweet reunion.

"It's going to be a hard few months," she nervously predicted.

I nodded, stood firm, and offered to let her finish what was left of my beer. She tipped it back. That was the day before I walked into my counselor's office and back out, no wiser. The crux came with what Annie said next. I was in the process of reassuring her—offering a new outlook, citing everything I'd learned before, during, and after my prison stint about seren-dipity and forgiveness—when she mentioned that the doctors could harvest eggs. "It's not covered by insurance," she added. Then she crushed the can as she delivered her wish to the cosmos, smiling as my manic heart began skipping beats. She said, "I think I want kids."

♦ ♦ ♦

Now I am sitting at a kitchen table, staring at those words on a computer screen, filled with a near-complete composition. There's a stack of bills nearby. Who knows? Maybe someone will read it. Hopefully many.

I've been debating the finish for hours. I could lie and say we both lived happily ever after, but the truth is I have no idea. Damned writer's block.

Five months have passed since the Maine ordeal. I've prayed for wisdom and even looked up Aishé on the internet; I scoured Facebook but haven't been able to find her, or *soarta*, anywhere.

What I do know is that Annie is upstairs puking her guts out. Today was her last treatment.

"Are you doing okay?" I ask her.

I hear her flush. She comes down the stairs with her bald head glinting in the first light of spring, shining through every open window.

"How do I look?" she asks raggedly.

I tell her, "You look absolutely beautiful." Same as always.

She rolls her eyes, but I swear to God and everything that I am serious. "We should celebrate," she says.

"Not the mountains," I beg.

Annie chuckles. She asks how the writing is going.

I'd really buckled down, made a concerted effort to fine-tune the process, regulated alcohol for the sake of coherency, and found the time while she was in the bathroom daily. It was either that or beg Paul to give me back my job, but I couldn't do it to myself and I couldn't do it to Aaron.

I tell her, "I hit a roadblock."

"Oh yeah? What's that?" she asks, puzzling. "Have you tried more beer?"

"Yes, of course I've tried it," I say. "It's no use."

"Where are you stuck?"

"The ending."

Annie smiles as if she'd known it all along. She goes to the fridge and brings out a lager, hands it over, and sits down at the table beside me. She closes my laptop, puts her hands on my knees, and says she wants to go to Las Vegas before the procedure—in vitro. The doctors said she could get pregnant immediately following chemo. But first, Annie wants to see the lights, and make wild gypsy love in the middle of some deserted highway beneath the stars.

"I'm sure that's a terrible decision, in light of everything," I say. I am thinking strictly in terms of certain consequence and inevitability: deadlines, her frail condition, and an unending pile of unpaid bills.

And she says, "My dear, this is only the beginning."